P9-DMR-682

JUDITH BLEVINS

KAMANDA

CARROLL MULTZ

OPEN WINDOW

Livonia, Michigan

KAMADA

Copyright © 2019 Judith Blevins & Carroll Multz

All rights reserved. Except as permitted under the U.S. Copyright Act of 1976, no part of this publication may be reproduced, distributed, or transmitted in any form or by any means, or stored in a database or retrieval system, without prior written permission of the publisher.

This book is a work of fiction. The characters, incidents, and dialogue are drawn from the author's imagination and are not to be construed as real. Any resemblance to actual events or persons, living or dead, is entirely coincidental.

Published by BHC Press
under the Open Window imprint

Library of Congress Control Number: 2018967629

ISBN: 978-1-948540-70-4

Visit the publisher at:
www.bhcpress.com

Also available in ebook

ALSO BY JUDITH BLEVINS

Double Jeopardy • Swan Song • The Legacy
Karma • Paragon

ALSO BY CARROLL MULTZ

Justice Denied • Deadly Deception
License to Convict • The Devil's Scribe • The Chameleon
Shades of Innocence • The Winning Ticket

ALSO BY JUDITH BLEVINS & CARROLL MULTZ

Rogue Justice • The Plagiarist • A Desperate Plea
Spiderweb • The Méjico Connection • Lust for Revenge
Eyewitness

Childhood Legends Series®
A series of novels for middle-grade readers
Operation Cat Tale • One Frightful Day
Blue • The Ghost of Bradbury Mansion
White Out • A Flash of Red
Back in Time • Treasure Seekers • Summer Vacation

CONTENTS

A NOTE FROM THE AUTHORS

The more we work on novels the more we find ourselves living the lives of our characters. They come alive and we have a difficult time separating fact from fiction. When they cry, we cry; when they laugh, we laugh. They seem to control what happens to them. We are mere scribes writing what our characters dictate.

Both of us have reached that point in our writing careers where collaboration is a preferred method of writing. We've made writing more of a social event than a self-imposed exile where writing is meditation being recorded. It's been said two heads are better than one and we find that to be true in writing our novels.

The current novel takes the reader on a journey that makes a convincing argument that you can fool some of the people some of the time but not all of the people all of the time. It also proves that deception comes with a price and that once you lose your self-respect you lose everything. To learn from the mistakes of others is always the preferred alternative.

To Margie Vollmer Rabdau and our publisher, BHC Press, our profound gratitude. Without them this novel would be just another novel.

...to the contrite of heart

Things are not always what they seem;
the first appearance deceives many;
the intelligence of a few perceives
what has been carefully hidden.

~ Plato ~

KAMANDA

1

WITHOUT A TRACE

WHEN WE ARRIVE at Denver International Airport Twyla Marin, my longtime secretary, is met by her husband Roy, a bespectacled, partially balding, unremarkable man in his late fifties. Roy helps Twyla claim her luggage and the two head toward the parking garage. I deliberately wait on the other side of the baggage carousel to further disguise the affair I'm having with Twyla.

I'm dismayed when Penny, my wife of over twenty years, fails to meet me at the prearranged time and location. After several unsuccessful attempts to reach her on her cellphone and at home I reluctantly grab a cab and head for home. We live on the Boulder County side of Erie. An entire section of land had originally belonged to my grandfather who later transferred it to my father who in turn transferred 160 acres to me. There Penny and I built a rambling ranch style home designed by Penny. Her whole life has been centered around her horses which I assume is the cause of me being stranded at the airport.

When I arrive home I open the door and call her name. When I get no response I make a sweep through the house looking for her. She's nowhere to be found. Her purse is in its usual place along with her car keys. I check the garage—no sign of Penny. Her SUV and my Mercedes are parked inside. They're both cool to the touch indicating they haven't been driven recently. Stormy, her favorite riding horse and several others are in the corral. None are lathered and none appear to have been ridden recently.

Surprisingly I'm in a panic. I hadn't divulged to Penny my plan to file for a divorce nor my wish that she would run off with another man and thus make our dissolution an amicable split. Our home was placed just in my name along with the 160 acres and without children there is no child support to worry about. Spousal maintenance or alimony, as it used to be called, is not a concern as Penny is independently wealthy due to an inheritance from a great aunt who was a spinster. Our prenuptial agreement provides a formula that pretty much dispenses with the usual property settlement wrangle.

I hurriedly change clothes and as I saddle Lover Boy I'm full of guilt at having cheated on Penny. Twyla is the opposite of Penny in looks and personality. She's tall and slender and favors the Nordic side of her family with blond hair, blue eyes and a light complexion. Penny, on the other hand, is of medium build, muscular and favors the Portuguese side of her family with dark hair, dark eyes and olive skin.

After riding around our property and not finding Penny, I unsaddle Lover Boy and put him back in his stall. I'm anxious about Penny so I use the phone in the stable to call Thelma Jorgensen, our closest neighbor and one of Penny's riding companions.

"Haven't seen or talked to her for several days," Thelma says in answer to my question. "Thought she might have made the trip to Cincinnati with you."

Now I'm really concerned when Thelma doesn't know where Penny is. They are as close as sisters and I know they confide in each other. As soon as I hang up the phone I dial 911.

Soon after my call two deputies from the Boulder Sheriff's Office appear at my door.

"Thank you for responding so quickly," I say as I usher them into the living room.

"We don't usually take a missing person report unless the person has been AWOL for seventy-two hours or longer," Deputy Lance Whittaker says.

"When was the last time you saw your wife?" Deputy Gretchen Fuller asks. Whittaker now has pen in hand and is poised to record my answer on a pad.

"Wednesday of last week. I was headed for Cincinnati to attend a book publisher's convention and she drove me to the airport. However, we spoke on the phone yesterday in the late afternoon and made arrangements for her to pick me up at DIA. Needless to say, she didn't show and wasn't home when I arrived here earlier."

"Have you tried her cellphone?" Fuller probes.

How dumb do I look? "Of course. I tried both her cell and the landline from DIA when she didn't show. No answer on either. You'll notice her cellphone's on the kitchen counter along with her purse." I point to her cellphone on the charger and her purse alongside it.

"Mind if I check her purse?" Fuller asks.

"Go right ahead," I say. "That was the first thing I checked when I couldn't locate her. I found her wallet and keys to the SUV inside her purse which caused me alarm."

Whittaker's ears perk up. "Locate her?"

"Yes, I do a lot of traveling and Penny never fails to pick me up upon my return at the prearranged time and place. When she didn't meet me at the airport today I took a cab home. I immediately checked the house, garage and stable. Both cars were in the garage so I assumed she was close, probably at the neighbors. I called her best friend, Thelma Jorgensen, who said she hadn't seen or talked to Penny for several days and thought Penny had accompanied me on my trip to Cincinnati."

"When you talked to Penny late yesterday, who initiated the call?" Fuller asks.

"She did," I reply.

"Then the call will likely be logged on the landline or her cell call record," Fuller says apparently as much for Whittaker's benefit as mine. All the while Whittaker is taking notes and peering at me as if I'm trying to build an alibi.

"Why do you ask?" I say wondering what difference it makes who called who and from what phone.

"If she called you from your landline that would mean that she was home at the time of the call which was less than twenty-four hours ago and her 'disappearance' not all that alarming."

"Her failure to show up at the airport and not telephone me or leave a note as to her whereabouts is alarming," I say. "If she had gone shopping she would have taken her purse and her SUV. If she had gone horseback riding one of the horses would be missing or if she had gone horseback riding and had been bucked off her horse, the horse would be lathered. If she had gone hiking on the property I would have located her. Don't you find all that rather alarming?"

"You make the trip to Cincinnati alone?" Fuller asks raising her eyebrows.

"No, my secretary, Twyla Marin, accompanied me. She helped me prepare the power point presentation I used in one of the sessions at the convention. Because of my ineptness with electronics I needed her to assist me."

"Was that a common practice?" Whittaker asks.

"When I'm part of the program," I reply.

Whittaker and Fuller exchange glances. "Was Ms. Marin more than a secretary?" Fuller asks and squints at me. Diplomacy is obviously not one of Fuller's attributes.

"No," I say. I don't like the insinuation so I add, "I'm happily married and so is Twyla. Our relationship is purely business." *Oh, my God. I hope Penny shows up to dispense with what appears to be mounting proof of a motive to cause her disappearance.*

"Nice home you have here," Fuller says. "Lived here long?"

"Almost twenty years," I say. "Before that we lived in Denver for a short time."

"Mind if I look around?" Fuller asks.

"No, go right ahead. Make yourself at home," I say.

"Wife seem happy here?" Whittaker asks as Fuller departs taking photos with her cellphone.

"She went to CU and always wanted to settle here. Being raised in Colorado she was enamored by country life."

"How did the two of you meet?"

"Penny was captain of the cheerleading squad at CU while I was captain of the football team. It was inevitable we would meet and fall in love."

Soon Fuller returns and joins in the conversation. "Didn't happen to have an argument with your wife when you last talked, did you?"

"She made insinuations about Twyla and me being joined at the hip and Twyla being more than my gal Friday—a topic that seems to surface every time Twyla accompanies me on one of my business trips. Other than that, we were civil towards each other and exchanged the usual 'I love you' at the end of our conversation."

"Any hint she would not be meeting you at the airport or that anything was amiss?"

"Just the opposite. In fact we made plans to go to Penny's favorite restaurant in Erie upon my return."

"That wouldn't have been Justine's by chance?" Whittaker asks.

"How'd you know?" I respond.

"I think it's everybody's favorite," says Whittaker.

As Fuller and Whittaker leave, Fuller advises me that she didn't find anything indicating a break-in and asks, "Were the doors to the house locked when you arrived home?"

"No," I respond, "which is unusual for Penny. She's a stickler when it comes to locking the doors when neither of us are home."

"Can you tell if anything is missing?" Whittaker asks.

"As far as I can tell things are just as they were when I left."

"With no evidence of foul play and considering the short period of time involved, I, for one, am hesitant to label this a missing person case," Whittaker says and looks at Fuller. Fuller nods.

"Here's my card," Fuller says.

"Keep us posted," Whittaker says and also hands me a card.

2

A CAUSE TO PAUSE

AFTER WHITTAKER AND Fuller leave I'm all alone and still feeling guilty. I begin to reflect on the disintegration of my marriage to Penny. It started shortly after I hired Twyla. That was five years ago—fifteen years into my marriage. My previous secretary, Mona Sanders, and her husband Larry decided they needed a friendlier climate and moved to Arizona. I thought Mona was irreplaceable until Twyla arrived on the scene.

Twyla was a sales rep for a textbook publisher whose home base was in Denver. Her husband, a dermatologist, tired of the fast-paced life in the city and moved his medical practice to Erie. The two settled on a five acre parcel on the outskirts of town not far from where Penny and I live. It was not long before Penny and Twyla became acquainted. Twyla shared Penny's love for horses and was soon boarding several of her horses with Penny.

When I began looking for a replacement for Mona, Twyla applied for the position. She was a natural and a valuable addition to Azar Publishers, Inc., a company I had founded upon our move from Denver. She was more than a secretary and more or less the manager of the firm.

In the beginning my relationship with Twyla was all business although Twyla and Roy were occasional guests at our home and Penny and I at theirs. During a convention Twyla and I attended in San Francisco our relationship evolved into a full blown

21

affair. Back home in Erie the affair hadn't cooled down and we found ourselves spending more and more time secluded from the watchful eyes of fellow employees and of course our spouses. Our excuses were creative and our deception most effective.

Deception was not in my DNA. Having grown up in a home where my father was a Lutheran minister and my mother a municipal judge, integrity was pounded into me along with the other virtues dictated by my parents' occupations. To tell the truth was more than in the oath my mother administered to witnesses in court and more than the Sixth and Tenth Commandments my father preached from the pulpit.

The Golden Rule was something I had adhered to for the better part of my life. "Do unto others as you would have them do unto you," made it easy to conform to the social norms and the mandates drilled into me by my parents. Much like Adam, despite the proscriptions imposed by my upbringing, I succumbed to a temptation, the consequences of which only the future will disclose.

For the past year the affair has become more than a series of random encounters with no strings attached. There's been a growing expectation on Twyla's part and an insatiable yearning on my part that propelled us into setting our eyes on a permanent arrangement. The only impediment has been our respective spouses. Since Twyla discovered her husband has been having an affair with one of the nurses at his clinic, she's been itching to return the favor. Also, she professes that I'm the love of her life and that she can't live without me.

Penny, on the other hand, is cold and indifferent. However, other than recent outbursts of jealousy over Twyla there has been little bickering between us nor has there been much love. Although I'm satisfied staying married to Penny while having the torrid affair with Twyla, almost fifteen years Penny's junior, Twyla has been becoming more impatient and the night before we left Cincinnati I was given an ultimatum—Penny or her. No more double dealing!

3

THE DREADFUL WAIT

ON MONDAY I'M at work early. Less than twenty-four hours has passed since I became aware of Penny's disappearance. I hesitated calling Twyla for fear my revelation might be misconstrued. In light of our pillow talk about shedding the old and heralding in the new I was reluctant to disclose that the problem on my end had ceased to exist.

My worst fears are realized early Monday morning when I tell Twyla that Penny has vanished without a trace.

"She what?" Twyla asks.

"Vanished without a trace," I reply.

"When?"

Twyla pulls away when I try to take her hand.

"Penny didn't pick me up at the airport so I took a cab home. She was not home when I arrived. However, nothing seemed to be out of the ordinary when I entered the house. Her purse, wallet and car keys were in their usual place on the kitchen counter. I was miffed as to why she didn't show up at the airport and called out to her. She didn't answer. Becoming concerned, I made a thorough search for her and even checked with Thelma. Thelma said she hadn't seen or talked to Penny in a couple of days and assumed she went to Cincinnati with me. I called 911 when it was apparent something was amiss."

"Her car and her horse?"

"Both her car and mine were in the garage and Stormy was in the corral. Guess we'll know fairly soon whether I'll need to file for a divorce."

"Not funny! Something horrible may have happened to Penny. And if she just ran off I'm not sure I can wait seven years to see if she returns." Twyla looks at me suspiciously. "You didn't have anything to do with her disappearance, did you?"

I'm stunned that Twyla would even ask that question. "Of course not! Why would you even think that?"

"You know!" There are now tears in Twyla's eyes.

When I try to comfort her she makes it clear she doesn't want to be touched. "We've both duped her—you her husband and me her supposed friend. If she comes to harm I'll never forgive myself." Twyla cries uncontrollably. I'm glad no one else has yet arrived at the office.

"But...I thought—" I reach for Twyla.

"Don't you dare touch me," she snarls and glares at me. "What did you do to Penny?"

"Nothing, dammit! I swear!"

"Well, you certainly don't seem to be very upset."

"How do you expect me to act?"

"I don't know. How can you be so cold, for heaven's sake?"

"She'll probably show up any time now. If not, at least half of our worries are over."

"But not that way!"

"It's not what you think. I had no hand in her disappearance and would do nothing to harm her."

"Have you called her parents? Perhaps she is visiting them or her sister in Colorado Springs."

"It isn't likely she would just take off without her purse, wallet or car. And yes, I've called them and everyone else I think may know where Penny might be. All I did was alarm them. They asked that if I hadn't heard from Penny by noon today to call them back and they would come immediately to assist."

"How about the authorities?"

"That was one of the first things I did after I found her missing. Two deputies showed up and looked around. The bottom line is that they refused to take a missing person's report for at least seventy-two hours."

Twyla paces back and forth in my office wringing her hands. "She's way overdue—call again!"

"I wanted to get your advice before I called them back…"

She grabs the phone, "If you won't call them, then I will!" she barks. Now I'm alarmed. Twyla sounds almost hysterical.

"Give me the damn thing," I say and grab the phone away from her.

She looks at me with a steely gaze, "Dial 911 and don't wait another second!"

I pull the cards Whittaker and Fuller left with me and call the Boulder Sheriff's Office. "Boulder County Sheriff's Office," a dispatcher says. "How may I direct your call?"

"This is Denton Ballard. I would like to speak to either Deputy Whittaker or Deputy Fuller, please."

"They won't be on duty until eight. Would you like to leave them a voice mail message?"

"Yes, please connect me with Deputy Whittaker's."

I leave a message for Whittaker to call me on my office phone. Twyla is on her way to her office before I relay the latest. I decide it's best to give her space to calm down. I pick up the phone again and call my home hoping Penny will answer. She doesn't. *How the hell did I get into this mess?*

I can't concentrate on my work which has accumulated in my absence. Jill Caragon, our receptionist, sorts and slices open the mail before distributing it. She's now at my door with a stack of mail.

"Thank you, Jill," I say. "Anything unusual happen during my absence? Penny didn't call while I was gone by chance, did she?"

"No, she didn't call but you did receive a package in the mail from her the day after you left for Cincinnati. It's on your credenza. I didn't open it thinking it was something personal."

When I turn and see the package a chill creeps up my spine. "Stay here," I say to Jill.

With Jill watching I rip open the package hoping it may be a clue as to Penny's disappearance. It's postmarked the day before I left for Cincinnati. I'm stunned when I look inside. It contains the stuffed panda bear I won for Penny at a carnival shortly after we started dating. Penny named it Kamanda in honor of her twin sisters Kay and Amanda who were several years younger than her.

When I remove the panda bear and show it to Jill she frowns but says nothing.

"Jill, this is the panda bear I won at a carnival when Penny and I were still in college. I threw a football through a car tire ten times without missing. She had a choice in the selection of a prize and picked this. Before presenting the panda bear to Penny I removed my fraternity pin from my jacket lapel and stuck it on the panda. I can still picture the look on her face." I notice a quizzical look cross Jill's face. She's probably wondering what this is all about.

"Does the panda have a name?" she asks obviously not knowing what else to say.

"Kamanda. Penny named it after her twin sisters."

I put the bear back in the box and break down and cry. I hate to admit that recently I had wished for Penny's disappearance and even considered for a brief moment the best way to get her out of my life in order to make way for Twyla.

"There now, Mr. B," Jill says and tries to comfort me. "Having problems at home?"

Embarrassed at my breakdown, I pull my handkerchief from my pocket and wipe my eyes. "Worse than that," I sniffle. "Penny has disappeared.

"Disappeared?"

"Yes, disappeared."

"What—."

"She did not meet me at the airport as prearranged so I took a cab. She was not home when I got there. She left behind her purse and keys to the house and her SUV. After I searched for her I called the sheriff's office. A couple of deputies came to the house but refused to label her absence a cause for concern. They said they couldn't take a missing person's report until she had been missing for at least seventy-two hours. Even though it's not been seventy-two hours I left another call for them earlier this morning." I pause briefly before asking, "Did you have any contact with Penny while I was gone?"

"The last time I saw her was on Monday a week before you left. She dropped off a bouquet of roses she picked from the garden. She was jovial when she came in. I asked if she wanted to see you and she said not to interrupt you that she knew you were busy. We visited briefly and she told me to have a good day then left."

"Did she appear to be distraught or upset?"

"No, not at all!"

I go to Twyla's office and tell her about the panda bear. She just gives me a blank stare. "Talk to the sheriff's deputies?" she asks.

"Haven't received a call back. You were there when I left the message. If I don't hear from them by ten I'll call back."

When I return to my office, Fuller is holding on the line.

"No word yet from your wife?"

"No, I've called anyone and everyone who might have seen or heard from her. I've reached a dead end and don't feel I will anytime soon."

"What makes you think that?"

"Wouldn't I have heard something by now?"

"Not necessarily. Guess we should have asked whether your wife had a history of disappearing or if you suspected her of being unfaithful."

"No to both questions. None of this makes any sense other than she ran off or is the victim of foul play."

There's an uneasy pause before Fuller asks, "Would it be possible for you to meet with Deputy Whittaker and me sometime today?"

"Yes, when and where?"

"How 'bout one thirty at the S.O.?"

"That'll work."

"In the interim try to think of anyone who might have a reason to harm you or your wife."

I cringe at the thought of going to the Boulder Sheriff's Office. I consider calling the company's attorney and having him or another member of his firm accompany me. I've heard some wild stories of how interviews turn into interrogations and statements into admissions that form the basis of a criminal prosecution. *Oh, what the hell! I haven't done anything wrong. Why the worry?*

When I arrive at the sheriff's office I see a waiting room full of anxious faces. There is a window with bars that has a slot at the bottom for sliding small items back and forth. Behind the bars is a uniformed deputy who must have been a drill sergeant at some time in her life. With short hair, the only hint that she's a woman is her voice. I stand in line waiting to respond to the gruff, "What can I do for you?" When it's my turn I announce I have an appointment with Deputies Whittaker and Fuller. I give her my name and she dials an extension and announces my arrival. She points to the seating area and tells me Deputy Fuller will be with me shortly.

"Just tell them you're not guilty by reason of insanity," a burly man sporting a Harley sweat shirt tells me. Another asks if I'm an attorney apparently since I'm wearing a suit and tie. I feel all eyes are peeled on me as I sit and wait and wait some more. I remove my jacket and observe that the dampness of my shirt is a dead giveaway that I'm nervous as hell. *Probably a telltale sign of guilt.*

"Mr. Ballard." The voice is that of Deputy Fuller. "Hope you haven't been waiting long." "Not at all," I say and resist the urge to look at my watch. Ten minutes ago I'd been waiting for thirty minutes.

I soon find myself in a room not much larger than a closet. The concrete walls are devoid of anything to soften the dingy gray paint. Whittaker does not bother to rise when I enter. Fuller points to a chair behind a metal table. She then sits on the chair across from me next to Whittaker. *I'm in an interrogation room!* My instincts kick in and now I'm on full alert.

Obviously noticing my discomfort Fuller says, "This is the only room available. It was a busy weekend especially with the

Buffs playing Stanford and emerging victorious. Things got a little wild on the home front."

"I understand," I say. "For a while I thought maybe I was a suspect and was looking around for the rubber hose and spot light."

The deputies' smiles do not reach their eyes. Not a good omen I conclude as the two seem to be all business.

Just as I suspect, the two assume the roles of good cop and bad cop. Fuller is the mean cop; Whittaker the sympathetic one.

"As you might imagine, Mr. Ballard, when a spouse mysteriously disappears his or her counterpart is the obvious suspect. In fact everyone is a suspect, especially family members and those closest to the missing party." Fuller raises her brows and peers at me in such a way that I'm now convinced I'm *the* prime suspect.

"I understand," I manage as I clear my throat. I don't remember being this nervous since I was brought before the principal in the third grade for shooting spitballs in class.

"People don't just up and vanish in thin air," Whittaker says. "Houdini maybe, but not a spouse."

"I agree. I don't know what happened to Penny. I had talked to her by telephone the night before I was to return home as I previously mentioned. There were no harsh words and everything seemed to be copasetic."

"You said your wife was upset over your relationship with your secretary and was not happy that you had taken her with you to Cincinnati for five days." Fuller is relentless. She should have been a trial lawyer. It is obvious she has made up her mind I'm responsible either directly or indirectly for Penny's disappearance.

"Twyla is a friend of both my wife and mine. For some reason Penny grew jealous of the relationship I had with Twyla and she let her imagination run wild with unfounded accusations.

I tried to dispel the notion by limiting my contact with Twyla outside the work place." It's then I suddenly realize that almost five days alone in Cincinnati with Twyla doesn't support my last statement.

"You didn't answer my question!" Fuller persists.

"I told you before and I tell you now my relationship with Twyla was purely business."

"Did your wife ever threaten to leave you because of Twyla or for any other reason?"

"No. Our marriage was more stable than most and neither of us ever threatened to leave the other. We slept in the same bedroom in the same bed. We had no reason not to trust each other and shared our secrets from the day we first met. We had a loving relationship."

"When was the last time you saw your wife?" Whittaker asks.

"On Wednesday when she dropped me off at DIA."

"Did she stay with you until you started through security?"

"No. Traffic is so hectic at DIA getting in and out is pretty much a hassle. I just had her drop me off at the departing passenger area."

"And you say you last spoke to her on Saturday the day prior to your return. Correct?"

"Yes."

"Remember what time that was?"

"Our last session ended somewhere around five p.m. I spoke to Penny before I cleaned up for the banquet that night. I was the featured speaker."

"I assume your secretary stayed at the same hotel," Fuller says with a smug look on her face.

"Of course. She attended the sessions with me and took notes. As I told you earlier, she assisted me with the power point presentation I made at one of the sessions and the speech I gave that night."

"You say this was a convention for Book Publishers of America?"

"I didn't say what the name of the association was?" I look at Fuller and raise my brows.

"We assumed that was the organization and confirmed that the national convention was held on the dates you indicated and that you had attended."

"Then you also know that I was the incoming president, correct?"

Fuller doesn't respond. Whittaker tells me to settle down. "Easy, Denton." *Whittaker is now calling me by my first name. Guess that means we're buddies.* "We're only doing our job. We'd be remiss if we didn't cover all the basis."

"Why the tape recorder?"

"Policy. We tape all our interviews," Whittaker responds. "I assume you have no objection."

Now's a great time to ask that question, halfway through the interview. "On the contrary. I have nothing to hide and want to have the record reflect that."

"You seem defensive," Fuller says.

"Wouldn't you be if you were in my shoes? I'm isolated in an interrogation room being grilled by two cops. I thought I was here to help you locate my wife, not to be subjected to the third degree."

"Whoa! Remember, you're the one who contacted us—not the other way around," Fuller responds. "If *you* were in *our* shoes, I assume you'd also be a little bit suspicious."

"I feel it's more than being just a little bit suspicious," I say.

"Perhaps at this point we should advise you of your constitutional rights."

"I already know what they are."

Fuller then pulls a card from her breast pocket and begins to read: "You have a right to remain silent. Anything you say can be used against you."

When she tells me I have a right to an attorney I assume the next line of questioning will delve further into my relationship with Twyla and her name so without any hesitation I invoke my right to have an attorney present.

I can see that Fuller is disgusted by the way she jabs the off button on the tape recorder and slams down the cover of her notebook.

The look on Whittaker's face tells me he's un-buddied me. "Have it your way," he sneers.

Before I call Azar's attorney to get a referral for a good criminal defense attorney, I stop by my office. Twyla is civil but withdrawn.

"I put some contracts on your desk for review," she says with a frosty tone of voice.

"Thanks," I say and can tell it's best that I keep my distance.

"How'd your interview go?"

"Looks like I'm the prime suspect in Penny's disappearance."

"How'd they arrive at that conclusion?"

"Apparently I was the last one to see Penny and the last one to talk to her."

"Did you call Penny's parents?"

"I called them earlier this morning and relayed the bad news. They're on their way as we speak and will be here sometime late afternoon. Penny's sisters, Kay and Amanda, and their husbands will be with them. Facing them is something I dread even more than being interrogated by the sheriff's deputies."

Twyla just stares at me.

"Why are you looking at me like that?"

She doesn't answer. After shuffling some papers around on her desk she asks, "What are you going to tell them if they ask if you and I are having an affair?"

"They already asked me that question and I told them 'no' that our relationship was purely business."

"What do I tell them if they ask me?"

"Same answer!" I'd think she could've figured that out.

Suddenly Twyla's attitude-shift alarms me. Her questions and silent stares are cause for concern. It appears she seriously thinks I did something to Penny. Twyla was my last refuge and now I'm feeling like a ship in a storm with no port in sight.

When Penny's family arrives, at first they are in denial that anything tragic could have happened to Penny. When I show them her purse and contents still intact and her SUV parked in the garage I watch concern evolve into hysteria and hysteria into grief.

Twisting a tissue in her hands, Gladys, Penny's mother, says, "Oh, dear me! It's not like her to just up and leave. Even as a teen she was usually thoughtful and usually told us where she was going and when to expect her to return home. I just can't believe she'd just...just..."

Harry, Penny's father picks up where Gladys leaves off. "Any evidence of foul play?" he asks.

Before I can answer, Kay, one of Penny's sisters chimes in, "The two of you have an argument?"

Amanda, Penny's other sister, chimes in, "She didn't get bucked off her horse and is lying somewhere out there, is she?"

All of these questions confirm my feeling that I'm a ship in a storm with no port in sight. It appears to me that they, too, now think I'm responsible for Penny's disappearance. I'm insulted that they would think I'm not savvy or caring enough to have explored all the possibilities and followed all the leads.

Curbing my anger, I say, "Even when Penny left for only a few hours, she always left a note. When she drove me to the airport on Wednesday everything seemed normal, and as was our habit, we kissed and exchanged 'I love yous' and that we would miss each other. When she called me the night before my return to Erie she said she could hardly wait for me to come home and that she would meet me at the airport. When she didn't, as I said, I took a cab home. She was nowhere to be found. I saddled Lover Boy and searched the property thinking she might have been thrown by her horse and injured."

When I told them about Penny having mailed Kamanda to my office while I was in Cincinnati, Kay's eyes lit up. "What an odd thing to do," she says. "Did you bring the panda back home?"

"It's in the master bedroom."

"Can I see it?"

"Of course."

Kay leaves and returns minutes later holding the panda. She has a strange look on her face.

"What's the matter?" Amanda asks.

Kay removes Penny's engagement and wedding rings from the hidden zipper pocket in the panda's body. She holds them up for all to see. "Penny would never leave home without these," she says.

When I see the rings I'm shocked. *What the hell! Why would Penny…this whole gig is mind boggling. Penny's up to something…*

My thoughts are interrupted when I notice everyone is staring at me. "I never thought to check the secret pocket," I say. Kay hands me the rings and I examine them. "Maybe Penny is trying to make a statement."

"What do you mean?" Gladys asks.

"Penny often accused me of having an affair with my secretary."

"Were you?" Harry snaps and glares at me as if the accusation was a fact. "Where there's smoke there's usually fire."

I'm between a rock and a hard spot. If I admit it, I've made my previous disclaimer to Fuller and Whittaker a lie. More importantly, I've just diminished myself in the eyes of Penny's relatives.

"No," I manage to say hoping they don't detect the deception in my voice.

"The grim reality is that for whatever reason Penny has called her marriage quits and has disappeared from the scene," Harry says. "At least there's hope that she just up and left you."

Harry smiles at Gladys. "Remember the summer between her junior and senior years in high school when she was unhappy for being grounded and stayed two days with a girlfriend?"

"Let's hope that's the case here," Gladys replies. "We know that Penny can sometimes be impulsive."

Wonder why they didn't mention that before!

"What's she doing for transportation?" Eric Banks, Amanda's husband, asks. "With no vehicle and her wallet and credit cards left behind she could still be here in Erie or maybe even in Boulder or Denver."

I nod. "She has a lot of friends and access to cash," I reply.

"Speaking of cash," Harry says, "have you checked your safe to see of anything is missing? I know the two of you kept a lot of cash on hand."

"No. Hadn't thought of that." I beckon for Harry to accompany me to the safe.

We head down stairs to where we keep the safe and steel filing cabinets which contain our personal records. When I flip on the light I see that the door to the safe is ajar. Penny was the only one who had the combination. The money she kept there, close to one hundred thousand dollars in large bills, was her insurance policy against the collapse of the banks.

"Well?" Harry asks.

I'm dumfounded when I see the money is missing. "There's not a dime left," I mumble. "The safe has been cleaned out."

I watch Harry's eyes narrow. "You don't suppose Penny was forced to open the safe by a burglar and was taken hostage?"

"Don't you think I'd have received a ransom note by now? Besides, everything else of value is untouched. Doesn't make sense that a burglar would focus only on the safe. Also, in light of the return of Kamanda with the rings intact, it's most likely the cash is her key to freedom."

When we break the news to the rest, I notice relief wash over them.

"My dear boy," Gladys sighs. "I owe you an apology. As impulsive as Penny can be, especially if she thought you were having an affair, it's more likely than not that her absence is a way of punishing you."

The next morning when Penny's family leaves, they all give me a hug and pledge to provide whatever assistance I need in discovering Penny's whereabouts. *At least for the moment I'm in their good graces. No telling how they'll feel tomorrow.*

4

GAME ON!

LLOYD SCOTT HAS been Azar's attorney since its inception. He and his wife Julie have been close friends of Penny and mine for many years. He's stunned when I inform him of Penny's disappearance.

"Any leads?" he asks.

"Not so far," I say. "Looks like I'm the prime suspect at least as far as the sheriff's office is concerned."

"Sounds as though you not only need my prayers but a referral."

"Yes, I do. Who would you recommend?"

"If I needed a defense attorney I'd call Willard Crowley. He's a senior partner at Crowley, Winford and Dickerson. He's the Perry Mason in this neck of the woods. Expensive but damn well worth every dime."

I'm not surprised as I expected that would be the case. I know there are cheaper lawyers out there but most of their former clients are behind bars. I ask, "Would you mind an intro? Although I've read about him and his high profile cases, he doesn't know me from Adam."

"I'll call him as soon as we hang up," Lloyd promises.

Sitting in the waiting room of the law offices of Crowley, Winford & Dickerson is like sitting in one of the offices at the Trump Towers. It is lavish not just by Boulder standards but by what I've seen in San Francisco and Washington, D.C. I can tell from the attorneys and staff who flow past that it's an efficient and sophisticated operation. Superiority permeates the air. Even though I'm dressed in an expensive suit, I feel out of place.

While my inferiority complex intensifies I remind myself that Penny's and my financial statements can rival any in this firm. I sit a little straighter.

A few minutes into my wait and after having completed the intake form, I'm approached by a tall, slender bespectacled younger woman who I assume to be a paralegal. She looks intelligent and I have no doubt that her I.Q. is double mine.

"Are you Mr. Ballard?" she asks.

"Yes, I am."

She leads me through a maze to Mr. Crowley's suite. When we enter Mr. Crowley comes around his massive executive desk and extends his hand. "It's a pleasure to meet you, Mr. Ballard. I understand you are an author as well as a book publisher."

"Sounds like you've been talking to Lloyd Scott."

"Yes, as a matter of fact I have. It appears your detective skills rival those of the protagonist in your new novel *Don't Give Me Tomorrow.* It's not often I run into a *New York Times* bestselling author."

"You may be representing one!" I say and manage a stingy grin. "Truth is I feel embarrassed about being here."

Crowley smiles, "I get that a lot. Sometimes I feel like a priest listening to a confession. Nothing surprises me and no sin is too great not to be forgiven."

When I address him by his formal name he says, "Just call me Will." I then relate the circumstances that brought me here.

"It's not unusual that the spouse and the last to see and speak with his or her missing counterpart is the prime suspect."

"I realize that. However, I thought an accused was presumed to be innocent. I feel as though I've already been charged, tried and convicted. And by the way I was interrogated it seems like they're not considering alternative suspects."

Will ignores my remarks and directs his attention to the form he's holding and asks, "On the intake form you list your age as fifty-seven. How old is your wife?"

"Penny's the same age."

"You say Penny left without her personal items including her identification and also left without her vehicle?"

"Yes and that's why I tried to file a missing person's report."

"Have you checked your joint bank accounts to see if any unusual amounts were withdrawn recently?"

"Did that yesterday. No funds were withdrawn. When I checked the home safe with Penny's father we found the door ajar and the safe empty. Penny didn't trust banks after the savings and loan scandal and she kept a large sum of money in the home safe. Penny called it her insurance policy."

"Do you have an estimate of how much money was in the safe?"

"In the neighborhood of a hundred thousand."

"Hmm. Anyone could have taken it. Either Penny or an intruder."

"Only Penny had the combo. The contents were mainly hers."

"An intruder may have forced Penny to open it."

"If there had been an intruder, why wouldn't they have taken the money in Penny's wallet and Penny's jewelry?"

"Good question. Was any of Penny's jewelry missing?"

"None that I could tell."

"What do you think happened to Penny?"

"After being told by her parents that Penny had run away from home when she was in high school, I'm led to believe she's capable of disappearing without a trace. She was impulsive and did things when she was angry."

Will kicks back and places his feet on his desk. His casualness makes me feel more relaxed. "Did the two of you have an argument before you left for Cincinnati?"

Déjà vu! That's about the tenth time I've been asked that.

"She was upset that my secretary accompanied me to Cincinnati. Even though Twyla was one of her good friends, Penny was envious of her and often accused me of having an affair with her."

"And were you?"

I hesitate to respond since I've denied any romantic involvement with Twyla—first with Penny and then the authorities. "Do I have to answer that?"

"If you want me to effectively represent you, you do!"

When I don't respond, Will says, "Remember, what you tell me is privileged. I can't divulge that information without your consent. That includes anything you tell me today even if you don't engage my services." Will peers over his glasses at me waiting for an answer.

Reluctantly I say, "Yes. I've been having an affair with Twyla for the last two and a half years." I shake my head and look down.

"Is Twyla married?"

"Yes."

"The two of you ever discuss divorcing your spouses and becoming a thing?"

"Yes."

"Of getting rid of your spouses?"

"Not in the context you infer."

"And what context is that?"

"That we would bypass the legal system and take the law in our own hands so to speak."

"Well put!" Will waits for an answer to his initial question.

"I would never harm Penny."

"I assume that means you are not responsible for Penny's disappearance?"

"Absolutely not! I would be willing to take a hundred polygraphs if that would prove my innocence."

"We'll discuss polygraphs later. Before we get there I need to ask some questions the answers to which may prove your innocence."

"I thought an accused didn't have to prove his or her innocence."

"That may be true in theory but the jury will expect you to dispel the inferences of guilt. So will the authorities if they're predisposed to file charges."

"I'm sorry. I've just grown cynical and frustrated because I haven't heard from Penny. I'm also upset with myself for having had an affair with Twyla and having deceived Penny."

"Other than Penny being impulsive and capable of leaving you in the lurch, what other evidence do you have to suggest she left of her own volition?"

When I tell Will about the panda bear his eyes light up. Up to now his note taking has been rather sparse.

"You say the panda bear arrived in the mail. Do you know when and where the package was mailed?"

"It was mailed in Boulder the day before I left for Cincinnati."

"You say the return address label was Penny's?"

"Yes."

"Did you save the packaging?"

"Unfortunately not. I didn't know its significance until now. Jill Caragon, our receptionist, can establish when the package was logged in and what it contained. She's the one who placed it on my credenza."

"I assume you recognized Penny's handwriting on the package."

"Absolutely. Penny definitely was the one who wrote the address label."

Will places his glasses on his desk and massages the bridge of his nose. "What did you do with the panda?"

"I took it home and placed it back on the dresser in the master bedroom where Penny kept it."

"Uh-huh. Why do you suppose Penny mailed you the panda?"

I squirm and cross and uncross my legs trying to get comfortable. "I won the panda for Penny at a carnival when the two of us were still in college. She named the panda Kamanda after her twin sisters Kay and Amanda. It was a symbol of my budding love for Penny. In fact I attached my fraternity pin to the panda before I gave it to her. Guess you could call our relationship puppy-love at that stage. Later when asked what she cherished most she would always say Kamanda."

"Why do you suppose she sent it to you and timed it so it would arrive in your office *after* you left for Cincinnati—a time when she knew you would be out of town?"

"I've given that a lot of thought. By returning it she was conveying that things were over between us. Actually, when her family was here yesterday her sister Kay asked to see Kamanda. She checked the secret pocket and found Penny's engagement and wedding rings. That was when I was convinced Penny was still alive and not the victim of foul play."

"How do you explain Penny leaving behind her personal items?"

"Looks like she wants me to know she's purging every memory of our lives together completely out of her life. Besides, she can always get a new driver's license and become established somewhere else. One hundred thousand dollars and who knows how much more can tide her over for quite a while. She's financially independent and doesn't have to work. That eliminates the possibility of background checks and the filing of bogus W-2 and Social Security forms. By making it look like I'm responsible for her disappearance she's counting on the hell I have and will continue to have. No telling what other surprises she has in store for me."

"Would she do that?"

"In light of the fact that she thought I was cheating on her, I think she would. She is pretty vindictive. She always finds ways to even the score."

"She put a lot of effort into her alleged disappearance. Why such an elaborate scheme?"

"I remember watching *Crime Stories* with Penny. In one episode the victim's husband was having an affair and was charged with having killed his wife even though no body was found. Out of the blue Penny said, 'Wouldn't it be funny if the wife deliberately disappeared just to make it look like her husband killed her?' I remember replying, 'It would be poetic justice. Life imprisonment for cheating on your wife.' 'Don't think it would warrant the death penalty?' Penny asked. I don't remember my response. But my point is: isn't that the exact thing that's happening here?"

"Unless the defense opens the door, what your wife said would not be admissible in court. Since she's not here affording us the opportunity to contradict it, it would be considered hearsay and inadmissible in court."

"How about Kamanda?"

"Kamanda may be your ticket to an acquittal!"

When I return to my office, I have an envelope with just my name sitting in the center of my desk. I recognize Twyla's handwriting. I open the sealed envelope and retrieve a one page handwritten letter. The further I read the more infuriated I become. The letter reads:

It is with heartfelt regret that I submit my letter of resignation effective immediately. After careful reflection, it is the only honorable thing to do. I cannot continue to live a life packed with lies. It is not fair to either Roy or Penny.

I am as much to blame for me having cheated on Roy and you on Penny. Penny was my friend and she trusted me though she shouldn't have. I never meant to lead you on and certainly didn't want our relationship to evolve into a serious one. Call succumbing to your charms a change in life and a desire for the attention that being married to an M.D. had denied me.

Penny's disappearance causes me grave concern. Whether she found out about us and fled or you had a hand in causing her disappearance I don't know. I do know that I do not want to condone in any way a diabolical plot to eliminate my competition. I'm troubled by your comment about one-half of the impediment to our relationship having been removed. I hope it doesn't mean what I think it means.

Please destroy this letter after you have read it and do not attempt to contact me.

Twyla

It's obvious Twyla is having second thoughts. As convincing and shrewd as Twyla is, it's not inconceivable that *she's* the cause of Penny's disappearance—either directly or indirectly. Chances are she kept a copy of the letter she sent me as an insurance policy should she become a suspect. She knows I won't be producing it since it establishes a relationship I've denied and asked her to deny.

When I meet with Will and hand him the $25,000 retainer I bring with me Twyla's letter. He reads it and shakes his head.

"Who else knows about your affair with Twyla?"

"Other than supposition by Penny and the employees at Azar, no one else."

"Are the authorities aware of the affair?"

"When I was interviewed the first time, Fuller and Whittaker asked if Penny and I had had an argument before I left for Cincinnati. I told them other than Penny's incessant accusations concerning my relationship with my secretary and her reaction to my secretary accompanying me on my planned trip to Cincinnati, everything was amicable."

"Did they ask for her name?"

"No and I didn't mention it."

"I assume they asked the sixty-four thousand dollar question: *Were* you having an affair with your secretary?"

"Of course and my answer was an unequivocal no."

"Other than me and of course Twyla, is there anyone else who is aware of your affair with Twyla?"

"Only suspicion as I've mentioned. Both Twyla and I have kept our affair a closely guarded secret."

"Even though you didn't mention Twyla by name she obviously would be on law enforcement's radar either as a possible suspect or witness. If she aided, abetted, assisted or encouraged you in any way she would be just as guilty as you. At the very least she would be a key witness against you. Her testimony that the two of you were having an affair would prove that you lied to police and if you testify in court your testimony would be suspect. More importantly, the fact that you were having an affair would establish *motive* for wanting to rid yourself of your wife."

"Do you think they've already interviewed Twyla?"

"The letter sounds like something a law enforcement officer might draft." Will raises his brows and peers at me.

"I thought of that. Why do *you* think so?"

"They've obviously made Twyla aware that she's a suspect and that if she cooperates in tying the noose around your neck she'll be off the hook. If they can get you to contact her they'll bug the conversation and use your statements to provide all the ammunition they'll need to convict you."

"Appears I'm damned if I do and damned if I don't."

"Only if you contact her and make damaging statements. It's possible she may contact you and try to meet with you under the pretext of reconciling. She of course will be wired and your incriminating statements recorded. Don't fall into that trap. It's an old ploy that has sealed the fate of many an unsuspecting target of the police."

"I haven't given up on Penny. Every time the phone rings I think it's her."

"Sounds like the S.O. has been waiting as well. It's been less than a week since anyone has heard from Penny."

"I expect they'll be knocking on my door anytime now with an arrest warrant of some kind."

"I'd like to head that off if at all possible. If you're still willing to take a polygraph I can make arrangements."

"What if I don't pass?"

"Then we don't need to disclose that to the DA. Innocent people sometimes flunk the exam and those who are guilty sometimes pass. It depends on the individual and how they react to being hooked up to a machine. Blood pressure, respiration and pulse rates vary and not everyone reacts the same."

"And if I pass, which I know I will, then what?"

"Then we present it to the DA in an effort to convince him not to file charges or if he has already filed charges to dismiss them since polygraph results are not admissible in court. Their only value is of a psychological nature."

"What charges would I be facing?"

"First degree murder, filing a false report, destruction of evidence possibly and obstruction of justice."

"I overheard Fuller and Whittaker talking about a polygraph."

"You don't want a polygrapher employed by the sheriff's office. They seem to find deception more often than a private polygrapher. Our office uses Curtis Dawson, a retired polygrapher from the Boulder P.D."

The next day I find myself hooked up to an instrument that looks innocuous enough to make me question its accuracy. I'm told to answer yes or no to the questions."

"Is Penny Ballard your wife?"

"Yes."

"Did your wife disappear?"

"Yes."

"Were you responsible for your wife's disappearance?"

"No."

"Do you know whether your wife is alive?"

"No."

"Do you know whether your wife is dead?"

"No."

"Do you know what happened to your wife?"

"No."

"Was your wife alive when you last saw her?"

"Yes."

"Do you know of anyone who may have wanted to harm your wife?"

"No."

"Did you want to harm your wife?"

"No."

"Have all your answers been truthful?"

"Yes."

Dawson repeats the test scrambling the order of the questions. My answers are the same.

Dawson unhooks me and removes a graph from the machine. In approximately thirty minutes he returns with a marked-up graph.

"I found no deception," the balding, frail man says. "That means you passed the polygraph! Here's a copy of my report." He hands the copy to me and says, "I'll email a copy to your attorney."

"The results are our ace in the hole," Will says. If Penny doesn't turn up and the authorities determine it is unlikely she will, they'll be hard pressed to solve the riddle of her disappearance. With you having been the last person to see Penny alive and having the motive to remove the major impediment to a permanent relationship with Twyla, you are the obvious fall guy. However, with no body and the possibility Penny may still be alive they have an uphill battle. And with you now having passed the polygraph, their prosecutorial decision to file charges is compromised."

"Don't they need a body to prosecute?"

"You're referring to what is called in the law the *corpus delicti* or body of the crime. In a murder prosecution it doesn't mean there has to be a body *per se*. If the circumstances are such that the available evidence points squarely to the accused such as DNA or fingerprints left at the scene of a murder or the murder weapon is traced directly to the accused, that is called circumstantial evidence and is considered the *body of the crime*. Otherwise every murderer who successfully disposes of the body of his or her victim is home free."

"How do they know Penny didn't stage her own disappearance to even the score for me having cheated on her?"

"That's why a murder prosecution without a body is always problematic. Again, the likelihood or unlikelihood that Penny staged her own disappearance will be a deciding factor in determining whether to prosecute without a body and ultimately whether a jury will convict should your case go that far."

5

THE ACCUSATION

WHEN MY PARENTS return from their ocean cruise, I tell them about Penny's disappearance.

"Why didn't you tell us sooner?" Mom scolds.

"Didn't want to spoil your vacation," I say.

"Nonsense!" Mom says. "You knew how to get in touch with us."

"It's only been a week since you left on your cruise and Penny has been gone less time than that. I keep expecting she'll show."

"Is the FBI involved?" Dad asks. "Chances are she's left Colorado and may be in Canada with Megan Frey. Have you tried to call Megan?"

"I've called everybody including Megan. No one has seen or heard from Penny. If anyone would hide her or know her whereabouts *it would* be Megan."

"Penny spends a week every summer with Megan at Prince Edward Island," Dad says. "I'd wager that if she's not with Megan, Megan knows where she is. They've been best friends, Penny often brags, since the first grade."

"Penny left without her wallet or SUV and without leaving a note of any kind. Even Thelma, one of Penny's riding companions, doesn't know where she is."

"Surely, she'd have said something to Thelma," Mom says. "To up and leave like that is not like Penny."

"Apparently she pulled a similar stunt in high school after she and her parents had an argument. So, who knows?"

"The two of you have an argument before you left for Cincinnati?" Dad asks and squints over his bifocals at me.

Just like when I was a child I cringe under his gaze and mumble, "Penny wasn't happy that Twyla made the trip to Cincinnati with me."

"I wouldn't be either," Mom snorts. "Why the way Twyla flaunts her body and flirts with every male who crosses her path I can see why Penny might be suspicious."

In my own defense I say, "Twyla has been a valuable addition to our firm. In fact I don't know what I'm going to do without her."

Mom jerks her head up and says, "Don't tell me she's disappeared, too!"

"No. She quit last week shortly after Penny disappeared."

"That seems odd," Mom says and looks at Dad.

I examine my palms for a brief moment then say, "She thinks I had something to do with Penny's disappearance."

"Oh, for Pete's sake! You didn't, did you?" Mom asks and looks at me sternly.

I'm abashed that she would even ask that. "Of course not," I say. "Why would I do that?"

"Well, from what you said, quite obviously to be with Twyla," Mom glares at me.

I come out fighting. Hoping to put them on the defense, I say, "I guess you think Twyla and I were having an affair?"

"You tell us," Dad says and firmly places his hands on his hips.

"I…I…" I can't admit to my parents I was cheating on Penny. Yet, I can't lie to them either.

Feeling cornered, I finally admit it. "Go ahead and disown me. It won't be long before everyone does. I *was* having an affair with Twyla." I break down and sob.

Dad puts a comforting hand on my shoulder, "Settle down, Denny, we believe you had no hand in Penny's disappearance. The question is will the authorities believe it when they find out about you and Twyla?" Dad shakes his head apparently in disgust. "Why would you jeopardize your marriage and your career over someone like Twyla? What the hell were you thinking?"

Dad's words were stinging. *What the hell was I thinking?* I risked it all and for what? In my heart I knew the little charade wouldn't last and that there would be a day of reckoning. I deserve whatever fate awaits me.

It's while in this frame of mind that I receive a call from Will.

"Denton, good news and bad news. This afternoon I met with Arthur Debow, our district attorney. Art was in my law class at CU. I gave him the results of the polygraph and we discussed your case. He was already aware of the ongoing investigation being conducted by the Boulder County S.O. He told me he's been waiting to make a decision until after all the witnesses—or at least the critical witnesses as he called them—have been interviewed. He also wants to make sure Penny's absence is not temporary."

"What was the good news?"

"He agreed to convene a grand jury and let a grand jury decide whether criminal charges should be filed."

I don't know how involving a grand jury is good news. Sounds pretty ominous to me. "What happens at a grand jury?"

"Boulder has a sitting grand jury consisting of twelve citizens of Boulder County. They evaluate evidence presented by the

DA's office and make the decision whether or not to charge. It's not left up to the DA. They have subpoena power and can require appearances from a wide range of potential witnesses including the targets of their investigation."

"Since I'm the prime suspect I assume I'll be subpoenaed."

"Hmm. Not necessarily. It depends on the evidence against you. If called, you could claim the Fifth. In other words, an accused is protected by the Fifth Amendment to the U.S. Constitution from being required to testify and making incriminating statements."

"But I have nothing to hide. I didn't do anything to harm my wife."

Will raises his brow, "The DA would have a heyday over your affair thus giving you a *motive* to rid yourself of your wife. If you testified before the grand jury you would be giving leads and information they would otherwise be unable to obtain."

Suddenly I'm short of breath. "I suppose they can call Twyla?"

"Most certainly. Not only can they but they will. The DA has already interviewed Twyla and not only has she admitted to the affair but has provided some very incriminating information such as you instructing her to deny the affair. The most damaging evidence is your telling Twyla that with Penny no longer in the picture one-half of the impediment to a permanent relationship had been removed. The DA was also provided with a copy of the letter she sent you."

I'm stunned and can't even respond. I just sit and stare at Will. After a long silence I ask, "Did you tell him about Kamanda?"

"Indeed I did. He said you could have mailed it to yourself, or if Penny mailed it, you were so enraged that you took Penny's life."

"And the rings Kay found in the secret pouch?"

"I hesitated telling him about those but knew his investigators would be interviewing Kay and would find out anyway. When I mentioned the rings, he said you could just as easily have removed them from your dead wife's hand after you killed her and put them in the secret pocket knowing they would be discovered."

"What you're telling me is that I'm dead in the water. So why is the grand jury considered good news?"

"If we leave the charging decision up to the DA you're SOL. With the grand jury we find out what evidence they have against you since we'll be receiving a copy of the transcript of all the witnesses' testimony if they return an indictment. Being forewarned is to be forearmed. With no body and no evidence that Penny is deceased a grand jury might refuse to indict."

"If they don't indict can the DA still files charges?"

"If the grand jury doesn't indict, the DA may be reluctant to file charges particularly with no proof of death and you having passed the polygraph."

Still confused I ask, "What happens if I'm summoned to testify before the grand jury?"

"As I said before, you seal your fate if you do. The thing you don't want to do is give them leads and statements that can be used to impeach you at trial if you testify. It's a no-win situation."

Great! If it's a no-win situation then why do I need Will? When I frown at Will he says, "The grand jury does not determine whether you're guilty or not guilty like a trial jury—only whether there is enough evidence to charge you. It doesn't take much. As far as they're concerned you had the means, opportunity and motive to eliminate your wife."

I'm losing hope. "I suppose Twyla's testimony would be enough for the grand jury to find a reasonable basis to charge."

"Right you are. If the grand jurors watch the cop shows, about every other episode involves someone who kills his or her spouse to make way for the spouse's replacement or to collect the proceeds from a life insurance policy or to bypass a divorce in order to avoid having to part with property or pay alimony."

"If I staged her disappearance to cover having eliminated my wife through some criminal means, then why wouldn't I have disposed of all her personal belongings when I disposed of her body? And why wouldn't I have driven her SUV to some remote location and maybe made our home look like it had been burglarized and Penny the victim of an abduction?"

Will just stares at me. *Is he thinking I wouldn't have been clever enough to have staged the scene and thought all of this out before killing Penny?* He clears his throat and asks, "Were you the sole beneficiary of Penny's life insurance policy?"

"No. Her twin sisters, Kay and Amanda, were the beneficiaries."

"How much was her policy?"

"A hundred thousand."

"Did you stand to inherit any property upon her death?"

"The cars were in joint tenancy as was our checking account and a savings account."

"How much was in the two accounts?"

"Roughly seventy-five thousand."

It suddenly dawns on me that if the DA asks all of these questions about how much I'd inherit upon Penny's death, coupled with the other evidence, how could the grand jury not indict?

"How about your business? I take it it's a corporation and that the stock is held in just your name."

"Correct."

"What value do you place on the stock?"

"About two million."

Will examines his notes. "You said that Penny had inherited some money from an aunt and that the two of you had a prenuptial agreement."

"She was independently wealthy and her inheritance was considered separate property as was our home and one hundred and sixty acres that was considered my separate property."

"It's unlikely she would have been awarded any alimony in the event of a divorce. So that would not be a reason to kill Penny."

As the picture unfolds I'm feeling more and more uncomfortable. "It looks like there would still be reason enough to eliminate Penny—at least as far as a grand jury is concerned."

"Did you share any of that information with Twyla?" Will asks and raises his brows.

"Dammit, of course I did when we were discussing a future together. That was before she threw me under the bus."

"You don't think Twyla had a hand in Penny's disappearance, thinking with Penny out of the picture, she would stand in Penny's shoes financially and otherwise, do you?"

That sounds more like a statement than a question. "That's a possibility considering her letter. She's now back-peddling and diverting the attention away from herself. It's always been just about Twyla. Roy is Twyla's third husband and she has bragged about taking her first two husbands to the cleaners."

"She would have the perfect alibi since she was with you during Penny's disappearance. As cunning as she appears to be she could have hired someone else to do her dirty work."

"I was so caught up in my situation that that never occurred to me. I wouldn't have thought it. But it certainly is a possibility. Appears I'm not the only one with a motive."

"The DA wants you to testify before the grand jury," Will says. "He also says you are the prime suspect."

Hearing the words *prime suspect* unnerves me. "What did you tell him?"

"I told him if he subpoenaed you, you'd invoke your Fifth Amendment rights against self-incrimination. Debow said he would subpoena you and have you state that on the record in front of the grand jury. After a little haggling he agreed not to do that so as not to taint the decision of the grand jury in deciding whether or not to indict. A lesser prosecutor would have you do that and thereby convey to the grand jurors that you must be guilty or otherwise you'd jump at the chance to proclaim your innocence."

"I assume Twyla is the only witness the DA will need in order to get an indictment?"

"With Fuller and Whittaker along with Twyla, they'd have their probable cause for an indictment. Your credibility would also be called into play with Twyla testifying as to an affair and Fuller and Whittaker testifying as to your denial."

Fighting depression and desperation I try to remain calm but I don't see how this could ever come out in my favor. "What do you anticipate I'd be charged with?"

"As I stated before first degree murder, concealing a death, false reporting and obstructing justice. All are misdemeanors with the exception of first degree murder which is a class one felony carrying a possible penalty of life imprisonment or death by lethal injection."

Will is so nonchalant when he lists the possible charges and penalties that I almost laugh. Life imprisonment or death by lethal injection are just words to him. However, they describe what my future holds in store for me. This has got to be a bad dream…

"Who decides the penalty for the first degree murder charge?"

"The jury who renders the guilty verdict."

Desperation clouds my reasoning and for a moment I consider fleeing the country so I ask, "If I'm indicted for first degree murder, can I bond out?"

"If the proof is evident and the presumption of guilt great, the court can deny bail. Otherwise, it is a bailable offense."

"And in my situation?"

"The proof is anything but evident and the presumption of guilt is iffy. I don't think Debow would oppose you being released on bail. When I spoke with him he was anything but confident in getting the grand jury to indict let alone getting a conviction."

Maybe it's not so bleak after all if the DA has reservations. "Would the trial jurors be the same as the grand jurors?"

"No, and the criteria for obtaining an indictment and a conviction are as different as night and day. All that the grand jury needs to indict is probable cause or reasonable grounds to believe you murdered your wife. At trial, the jury has to be convinced you are guilty beyond a reasonable doubt. That's a much tougher burden."

By mid-week of the fourth week following Penny's disappearance, the grand jury returns its indictment charging me with first degree murder, concealing a death, false reporting and obstructing justice. I'm devastated. Guess I had my hopes up after my previous conversation with Will.

I keep waiting for Penny to return. I have been in daily contact with Penny's parents and they seem shocked by the indictment. My parents likewise seem shocked when I tell them.

At the bond hearing my parents post the $100,000 cash bond set by the court. My father curses the criminal justice system; my mother is also incensed. Me? I'm still numb wondering if all of this is nothing more than a bad dream.

My indictment, arrest and bail hearing hit all the local news outlets. The headlines of the *Erie Chronicle* reads:

LOCAL BUSINESSMAN INDICTED ON MURDER CHARGES

The front page story shows a photograph of Will and me exiting the Boulder County Courthouse amid the swarm of reporters from both the print and electronic media. The subtitle that follows reads: "Denton Ballard, founder of Azar Publishers, Inc., seen here exiting the Boulder County Courthouse following a bond hearing upon the return of an indictment by the Boulder County grand jury."

The lead story reads:

> Following a month long investigation in the disappearance of Denton Ballard's wife, Penny, the Boulder County Grand Jury has returned its indictment charging Ballard, president and founder of Azar Publishers, Inc., with first degree murder, a capital offense. The indictment also charges Ballard with concealing a death, false reporting and obstructing justice.
>
> The indictment was returned a month to the day that Penny Ballard was reported missing from her home. According to sheriff's office reports, Ballard reported his wife missing upon his return from a business trip to Cincinnati. Investigation revealed that Ballard's wife had left her wallet with identification, driver's license and credit cards together with her car keys behind. Her SUV was found by investigators in the garage. According

to the report there was no evidence of a break-in or foul play.

Bail in the amount of $100,000 was posted by Ballard's parents, Ted and Dora Ballard, of Erie. Investigation is still pending. Ballard is represented by Boulder attorney Willard Crowley. Arraignment on the charges has been set for 10:00 a.m. on Wednesday of next week. Judge Madeline Stockton continued Ballard's bond to that date.

People who I thought were friends stare at me when I do my shopping or fuel up my car. Mother insists on me having dinners with her and dad. Just as well. I'm a poor cook and need the company. So far Penny's parents and sisters haven't disowned me. Neither have my brothers, Aaron and Rusty. As far as my employees are concerned, they let me know they're behind me and glad to be rid of Twyla. Her coworkers have some choice words for her and names I cannot repeat. *Guess I was so infatuated with the she-devil I didn't see how she was affecting the rest of my employees. I just hope the revelation isn't too little too late.*

When I'm arraigned I'm advised of the charges brought against me and the possible penalties. I enter a plea of not guilty to all charges and as instructed by Will, a demand for a jury trial.

Judge Stockton has what Will describes as a *robe syndrome*. I guess her to be in her mid-forties. Attractive enough, Will says she uses intimidation to maintain order in the courtroom and to dissuade attorneys from challenging her rulings. Clicking her pen constantly is a bit distracting but my overall impression is that she will be fair and impartial. Setting my bond at $100,000 is indicative of that.

Arthur Debow reminds me of Alex Trebec, the host of the game show *Jeopardy*. When I mention that to Will he nods and says that he's never seen Debow wear the same suit twice. "However, I doubt that Debow, like Trebec, has fifty suits at his disposal. Don't let his gentlemanly manner fool you," Will warns. "He's a little bulldog and will pin you to the mat before you know it."

When I look around the courtroom I spot my mom and dad. They arrive too late to sit in the front row. The courtroom is filled with curiosity seekers and members of the media. Since cameras and recorders are banned there are few distractions.

I'm not as nervous as I was at the bond hearing. Being pinned up like a wild animal is not something I need to be worried about—at least not for a while.

"The court will accept your not guilty pleas, Mr. Ballard," Judge Stapleton says. "The court will set this matter for hearing on motions and each side shall have ten days from today's date to file appropriate motions. The attorneys are instructed to meet with my clerk to set a date for hearing on the motions. Until then this court will stand adjourned and Mr. Ballard's bond will be continued to that date."

"That was sweet and simple," I say to Will.

We make the front page of the next issue of the *Erie Chronicle*. The headlines read:

BALLARD ENTERS PLEA IN WIFE'S DISAPPEARANCE

The story that follows reads:

Denton Ballard, at yesterday's arraignment, entered pleas of not guilty to first degree murder, concealing a death, false reporting and obstruction of justice.

Penny Ballard, the accused's wife, has been missing now for almost six weeks. Her disappearance has baffled investigators. According to Boulder County Sheriff's reports, Penny Ballard, age fifty-seven, disappeared under suspicious circumstances. Her husband reported her missing upon his return from a business trip. According to a spokesperson from the Boulder S.O. her husband has been the prime suspect from the start. Shortly after his wife's disappearance, Ballard was indicted by the Boulder County grand jury for first degree murder and the three related charges.

When Ballard's attorney, Willard Crowley, was asked by a reporter from the *Erie Chronicle* what defense his client would assert, Crowley said: "Alibi. Mr. Ballard was in Cincinnati at the time of his wife's disappearance and has no knowledge whatsoever of her whereabouts and as far as he knows, she is still alive." When asked if Ballard's wife might have staged her disappearance, Crowley responded, "Anything is possible. Why my client was charged with murder when there is no body or evidence of foul play is baffling particularly since he passed a polygraph."

The prosecution and defense have ten days to file motions according to District Judge Madeline Stockton's order. Ballard's $100,000 bond has been continued to the motions hearing date.

6

MARIN v. BALLARD

I'M MORTIFIED BY the events as they unfold. Everything is surreal and I feel my ordeal has just begun. I'm more worried about Penny than myself. With the passing of each day my hope dwindles. I'm guilt ridden for having deceived Penny and pray she's not in harm's way. If I could turn back the clock two and a half years, I would opt to keep my marriage vows and be true to the love of my life—someone who I depended on and someone who depended on me. *May God forgive me!*

My thoughts are interrupted when Jill calls me from the front desk. "There's a deputy sheriff out here who says he has some papers to serve on you."

"Send him back!" I say as my stomach churns. *What now?*

When the deputy hands me the papers, I'm stunned when I see the caption on the summons and civil complaint. *Twyla Marin, Plaintiff v. Denton Ballard, Defendant.* As if I hadn't already paid the price for my indiscretion I now find myself on the civil end of a sexual assault/harassment case. As soon as the deputy leaves I dial Will's cellphone.

"I was just served with a summons and a civil complaint," I blurt before Will can even say hello.

"Don't tell me. Let me guess. Twyla has filed a sexual assault and sexual harassment case seeking a half million dollars in damages."

"How'd you know?"

"A few minutes ago I ran into Caleb Bidwell at the courthouse. He knew I was representing you in the criminal case and said he was representing Twyla in a civil action brought against you. I just barely got back to my office and was going to call you. Bidwell claims Twyla submitted to your advances to keep her job. He said they were seeking a quarter of a million dollars in actual damages for emotional distress, lost income and counseling fees. In addition, he said Twyla would be seeking punitive damages because of your egregious conduct."

"Everything was consensual," I say, "and her letter confirms that."

"According to Twyla it wasn't. What she claims is that over a period of years you subjected her to unwelcome sexual contact."

"What! That's a lot of bullshit!" *That lyin' bitch...* I rub my forehead in exasperation. "What'll we do now?"

"Bring the complaint over and let me review it."

When I arrive at Will's office, I'm clutching the paperwork in my fist. I'm still seething over the allegations of both the criminal and now the civil complaint. He cools me down by making me sit and wait in the reception area for a few minutes. When I enter his office, a tray with a bottle of Cutty Sark, two crystal highball glasses and an ice bucket are sitting on a coffee table. Will rounds his desk and motions me to a chair on one side of the table. He sits on a chair opposite me and pours a drink for each of us. We are silent for a few moments as we each take a sip.

"Let me see the complaint," he says as he reaches for it. I hand him both the summons and the complaint. I watch as he reads the complaint. He nods as he studies it. Peering over his glasses he says, "Appears you foisted yourself on Twyla for a number of years and she succumbed out of fear of losing her job."

"Actually, after having worked as my secretary for two and a half years, one afternoon she came into my office and closed the door. She came around my desk and as I looked up at her she leaned over and kissed me full on the lips. 'There's more where that came from,' she said. That was the beginning of a torrid sexual affair. She's the one who insisted on adjoining rooms when we travelled. It was she who came into my room to spend the night—not the other way around. Even in the letter I gave you she admits to being equally at fault."

"Are you sure she's the only one, other than yourself, who can verify that the two of you were having an affair?"

"We were careful not to make it appear either in the work-place or at social events that our relationship was anything but platonic. We never texted each other, wrote notes or sent cards for fear our spouses would find out. Neither of us kept diaries or kept a record of our encounters—at least I didn't and I doubt she did. The only ones I've told are you and my parents."

"How long did Twyla work for you?"

"Approximately five years."

"Did she ever complain or object to your advances?"

"Never. In fact she was usually the instigator and the one who wanted to elevate our relationship into a permanent one. She's the one who planted the idea—not me."

"Why did you hook up with Twyla in the first place?"

"She was fifteen years younger than me and I guess I was flattered by the attention of a much younger woman. Penny and I had settled into the boring ho-hum existence that comes with having been married for many years. There was no excitement left in our relationship. Twyla rekindled that first love feeling in me and I became addicted to her. The way men looked at her made me feel as though I had conquered Mt. Everest. Since I was not very popular in high school and had an inferiority complex most of my life, being with her made me feel like a celebrity."

"Did you ever use her employment as a lever to obtain sexual favors?"

I shake my head. "She worked for me two and a half years before the infamous Twyla kiss. Her salary increases were in accordance with company policy and she received no special treatment in return for what you call sexual favors."

"Why do you suppose she filed the civil action?"

"I'm wondering about that myself. I think it was probably to save her marriage. Knowing she would have to testify in the criminal case because of her testimony before the grand jury, she realized her husband would find out about the affair. To blame me for it exonerates her and provides the excuse for her having cheated on Roy."

"We'll know what her testimony was when we get the grand jury reports in the criminal case and if she tape recorded any of your telephone conversations."

"If she did—with the exception of those since Penny's disappearance—most will be guarded and if anything, will prove she was a willing participant. I've also given some consideration to the fact that Twyla may have had something to do with Penny's disappearance. After all, Penny's and my combined assets are nothing to be sneezed at."

"That's an interesting concept," Will says and looks up from his notes. "We'll need to stall the proceedings until after your criminal case concludes. That includes filing an answer. If they take your deposition in the civil case and/or you testify at trial in the civil case they can use any and all of your incriminating statements against you in the criminal case—even if you don't testify in the criminal case."

"You mean if I testify in the civil case and admit to having had an affair with Twyla they can use it in the criminal case?"

"It's an admission or statement against interest. By lying to the sheriff's deputies about not having an affair and then testifying that you did, the false reporting charge is a gimmie. It's no longer your word against Twyla's. It also provides motive in the criminal case."

"What happens if I don't testify in the civil case?"

"Then unless we get a stay because of your pending criminal prosecution, judgment can be entered against you."

I'm stunned. "In the amount of a half million?"

"Twyla still would have to prove damages. Without a stay we'd be required to file an answer to prevent a default judgment from being entered against you. In the answer, even though your affair with Twyla was consensual we'd have to admit to the affair. If we denied it, it would be perjury—a felony."

"I'm dammed if I do and dammed if I don't."

"As a figure of speech—yes!"

"Why don't I just hang myself now and save everyone the trouble?"

"Because you're not responsible for Penny's disappearance."

"Seems Twyla and everyone else thinks I am."

"Let me talk to Twyla's attorney and see if we can settle the civil case out of court. If we can, we'll know it was filed for her husband's benefit and perhaps to dispel the notion she had a hand in Penny's disappearance. If we can't, then we'll know it was probably for the money."

"Does that mean Twyla might not have to testify in my criminal case?"

"The DA will probably grant Twyla immunity and she'll be required to testify in the criminal case. Her testimony is critical in proving motive on the first degree murder charge and in establishing the elements in the false reporting and obstruction of justice charges. Without motive and no body the prosecution will have no case on the murder charge."

"What happens if Penny shows up after I've been convicted of first degree murder?"

"You asked me that before. If your sentence is not death by lethal injection and you've not been executed, then we obtain your release from prison and complete exoneration."

"Guess I have more than one reason to pray that Penny returns safe and sound—and the sooner the better."

"Amen to that. I'll try to meet with Caleb Bidwell and see if we can work out a settlement. How much are you willing to pay to make the civil case go away?"

"Let me give that some thought. The bitch doesn't deserve anything!"

"In the interim I'll seek a stay and temporary halt to the proceedings until after resolution of the criminal case. Our chances are good since they require you in essence to incriminate yourself in violation of the Fifth Amendment. That applies to the pleadings, discovery and trial of the civil case."

My head is spinning, this is all so confusing. "Can you at least file something to deny that I forced myself on Twyla and that the affair all along was consensual?"

"One of the allegations in the complaint is that you had an affair. If we respond we have to admit you *had* an affair. That admission could be used against you in the criminal case. As I said previously that would establish motive and an admission you lied to authorities."

"Looks like I've painted myself into a corner."

Will claps me on the back as we walk toward his office door. "That you have, my friend. That you have. I'll file the motion for the stay later today. Bidwell will probably oppose it and we'll have to have a hearing. Neither you nor Twyla will have to appear."

"Finally some good news," Will says several days later. "Judge Weber has granted the stay. Bidwell did not appear happy with the decision. Again, we can only speculate on the reason Twyla filed the suit in the first place."

"Don't think it was because of the money. Being married to a doctor hardly places her in the category of an indigent."

"I wouldn't be too sure. If Bidwell is working on a contingency he'll want to squeeze as much out of you as he can. That having been said, her motive is probably to dispel the notion that she might be involved in Penny's disappearance. When you mentioned one-half of the impediment to a permanent relationship with Twyla had been removed that apparently spooked her and she thought perhaps you might have done the unspeakable. If she watches the cop shows the prime suspects are usually the surviving spouse and/or the *paramour*."

"I thought Penny had left me and that was the reason for the remark. I still think that's what happened and the minute I've served a significant period of time in prison or been executed, she'll miraculously reappear."

Will smirks. Apparently he thinks I'm exaggerating. "Oh, come on, Denny. Do you really think she'd be that vindictive?"

Without hesitation I respond, "Absolutely! Hell hath no fury…"

Will finishes the cliché, "…like a woman scorned."

"Something that I've never mentioned to anyone is that shortly after our engagement Penny somehow found out that one of my ex-girlfriends had come to town and that we secretly ar-ranged to have dinner together. In the middle of dinner at an exclusive restaurant, Penny stormed in. She approached my ta-ble and ceremoniously tipped my dinner plate over onto my lap. When my date objected, Penny christened her with a glass of ice water. Penny was then seized and escorted from the restaurant by two of the waiters as she shouted expletives at the top of her lungs. She disappeared for almost a week. Later I found out she had been shacking up with one of her old boyfriends. She didn't deny it when I confronted her with it. In fact she said 'turnabout is fair play.'

"There were other incidents throughout our marriage that I don't want to get into. So yes, I think she'd be that vindictive."

"Enough to cause you all this grief?"

"Hell, yes! Penny always retaliated. Didn't matter how slight or how egregious the incident was, Penny exacted her pound of flesh—with interest."

"Hum—" Will says.

"I know what you're thinking. Why then was I dumb enough to get tangled up with someone like Twyla…"

"You a mind reader?"

"No, but obviously that's the question and I don't have an answer. Guess I wasn't thinking which seems to be my pattern. Penny and Twyla were good friends and our deception must have been too much for Penny. Other than shoot Twyla and me, she staged her disappearance to teach us both a lesson. I've been chastising myself ever since I made that fatal mistake."

"Well, Penny did a great job if indeed that's what happened."

"Yeah, I'll say. Did you and Bidwell talk about settlement?"

"I want him to come to me. With the civil case on hold for who knows how long he'll be desperate to reach a settlement. Having accomplished what she wanted Twyla will also want to rid herself of the case. If we appear anxious the ante will go up. Right now we're in the catbird seat."

"Bidwell is willing to settle the case for one hundred thousand dollars," Will says.

I gasp. "A little steep, don't you think?"

"Absolutely. I told him I'd pass on the offer but didn't think you'd agree. He knows the drill. He said for us to make a counter offer."

"If you're willing to settle for fifty thousand, counter with twenty-five."

It isn't long before Will calls back. "Game on, baby! Get out your check book. We've settled the civil case for fifty thousand."

"Guess they didn't want to wait for the criminal case to run its course. Besides, if I'm convicted Twyla may have a hard time collecting a hundred thousand from a dead man."

"Whatever the reason, that's one less trial we need to worry about."

"Worth fifty thousand to get Twyla off my back. Can't believe, like Adam, I agreed to eat the apple."

"History, even ancient history, repeats itself," Will says.

"How well I know. Deceit exacts its own price and does not go undetected for very long. As that old Midas Muffler add says: 'Pay me now or pay me later.'"

"It's something that keeps on paying!"

"Now I know what *payback is hell* feels like."

7

OUT OF THE BLUE

SEVERAL WEEKS HAVE passed since the settlement in the civil case and Will and I are able to concentrate on the criminal case. Will had obtained an extension to file motions in the criminal case and the hearing on the motions had been moved back. Needless to say Penny's disappearance still remains a mystery.

Out of the blue Twyla calls the office.

"Mr. Ballard," Jill says, "Twyla Marin is on the line and wants to speak to you."

I'm dumbfounded. *What nerve! This feels like another twist on the knife she thrust into my back.* "Twyla Marin," I say. "Are you sure?" *This could be a cruel joke and someone impersonating Twyla.*

"The caller identified herself as Twyla Marin and I recognize her voice."

"Tell her Judge Weber issued a no contact order and I'm obligated to follow it. I cannot under any circumstances have any contact with her." I hang up wondering what the hell Twyla has up her sleeve.

Moments later Jill is back on the intercom. "I told her what you said and she s insistent that she talk to you. She said the order didn't prevent her from contacting you."

"Tell her I don't think it's a good idea." I'm torn between curiosity and common sense. I'm relieved when Jill doesn't buzz me back. *Even with Jill as a witness to what just transpired, Twyla is so cun-*

ning she'd figure out a way to accuse me of violating the no contact order if it worked in her favor.

Approximately twenty minutes after the phone call, Jill is back on the intercom. "Mr. Ballard, Twyla Marin is here and wishes to speak with you."

I don't want Twyla to cause a scene so I reluctantly relent, "Show her back," I say, "and when you leave, don't shut the door."

When Twyla comes in and Jill leaves, Twyla looks over her shoulder and makes a show of noticing the door was left ajar. I ignore her indignation and motion for her to sit. She seems demure and sits on one of the chairs facing my desk. Neither of us speak for several awkward moments. Finally, Twyla says, "I don't blame you for not wanting to speak to me. I haven't exactly made your life easy."

I glance toward the door and it's comforting to know Twyla couldn't possibly make any false accusations about our meeting this morning. "What can I say after you threw me under the bus?"

I watch Twyla squirm. She finally says, "First let me apologize. Penny's disappearance has stressed me out since I'm partly to blame."

If I'd said that, the cops would interrupt it as a confession. Maybe I should be recording this conversation. I look around. Not wanting to alarm my staff, I suggest we meet at the Sunlight Coffee Station. Twyla nods and we walk out together.

We take separate cars and meet at a table in the corner. Renee, the waitress, calls us by name since Sunlight is a regular hangout for the coffee drinkers in our firm. Over Danish and fresh brew we start the conversation with casual discussion. It's not long before we're back on the topic of Penny's disappearance.

I'm on full alert and figure Twyla is a plant seeking admissions and maybe even a confession. My conversation is guarded and interspersed with self-serving statements—just in case everything is being recorded on her end.

"Have any idea where Penny may have gone?"

I try to disguise the are you kidding look that crosses my face. *If I had any clue I'd have told the cops a long time ago. This is feeling more-and-more like a setup.* I decide to play along. "Your guess is as good as mine. However, with her leaving behind her wallet and SUV I suspect foul play. Since some valuables are missing it's possible the intruder may have kidnapped her."

"You don't think Penny staged her disappearance?"

"No. Why in the hell would she do that?" I look at Twyla and raise my brows.

"To even the score."

"It appears you know Penny pretty well since you're best friends." I use the present tense for a reason. I'm conveying that I think Penny is still alive—which by the way I believe to be true. "You don't think Penny would be that vindictive, do you?"

Apparently my question catches Twyla off-guard. It feels like she was expecting me to do all of the speculating and for her to catch *me* in a trap. I watch her squirm again and suppress a smile. Even the small victories feel good.

"Not sure," she says in answer to my question. I notice we seem to be engaged in a new version of Russian roulette because Twyla is also guarded with what she says. I'm now convinced the authorities have granted Twyla immunity in exchange for her cooperation in getting me to sing. *Two can play this game!*

"Twyla," I say, "the thought occurred to me that you might have not only been the indirect but the direct cause of Penny's disappearance. Please tell me it isn't so."

Twyla blanches. Maybe that pull of the trigger landed on the cylinder containing the bullet. Score another one for the good guys. "You know I wasn't."

"Really? Just how do I know that—you need to tell me."

Twyla looks nervously around the coffee shop. She finally hisses at me, "Of course I wasn't."

"Nor was I. Funny, when I declare my innocence nobody believes me. Why do you expect me to believe you now? You even said you were partly to blame." Twyla just looks at me. She's apparently too stunned to say anything. I detect something similar to terror in her eyes.

"I need to get back to work," I say. When I get up to leave Twyla remains motionless. Wonder what those deputies who are monitoring our conversation are thinking. Maybe now they'll take the alternative suspect theory, as Will calls it, a little more seriously. Maybe Twyla wasn't a plant but she's certainly going to be called as a witness by the prosecution in the criminal case. Under oath, she's going to have to testify that I point plank questioned her involvement in Penny's disappearance. *Wonder how it feels to have the shoe on the other foot?*

❖ ❖ ❖

The next day I call Will to report my encounter with Twyla. "Just getting ready to call you but was interrupted by an urgent call from another client. Sheriff Bernie Lang called wanting to interview you in the disappearance of their star witness in your criminal case.

My heart skips a beat and I almost drop the phone, "Twyla Marin?"

"One and the same. Apparently her husband called 911 and wanted to file a missing person's report since she failed to come home last night."

"Why do they want to talk to me?"

"They think you might have had something to do with her disappearance."

I'm too numb to respond.

"I have an opening if you want to come in now," Will says.

"I'm…I'm on my way."

When I tell Will about my encounter with Twyla yesterday, he just shakes his head. "Of all the days to pick—the day Twyla disappears!"

Will's demeanor changes and he gives me a stern look.

"What is it," I ask.

Will shakes a forefinger at me, "In case Twyla returns and for future reference, as your attorney, my advice to you is stay completely away from her. The open office door was a good choice but then leaving with her was poor judgment. Travelling in separate cars is just your word. No one else can vouch for that. If seeing her for some reason is a matter of life or death, make sure you have one or better yet two other people present."

Feeling like an idiot for falling into the trap, I say, "I see your point." I'm mentally reliving our conversation in the coffee shop. Perhaps my implicating her in Penny's disappearance caused Twyla to *arrange* her own disappearance—thus leaving me holding the bag.

"I can establish an alibi for the day. Twyla came into my office at about ten thirty. We arrived at the coffee shop about eleven and were there less than an hour. We arrived at the coffee shop and left the coffee shop in separate vehicles. Since it was almost lunch time I went home and fixed a sandwich and a bowl of soup. I was back at the office around one."

"When you say you had an alibi, what about the period between twelve and one?"

"Like I said, I went home for lunch."

"Did you go home alone?"

"Of course."

"Who can testify you went home for lunch?"

I scratch my head. "I see your point. Since our house isn't very close to others in the vicinity, I'm not sure if any neighbors could testify they saw my car in the driveway."

"The Achilles heel is that one hour window."

"Jill can testify as to Twyla's telephone call and Twyla coming into the office."

"She can also testify the two of you left together at eleven and you returned to the office alone around one."

"Our waitress, Renee Stapleton, can testify we were at the coffee shop from eleven to a little before twelve."

"She can also testify that the two of you left together but she can't testify as to what the two of you did after you left the coffee shop."

Will is beginning to unnerve me. "Sounds like you think I had something to do with Twyla's disappearance."

"Not in the least. If I did, you wouldn't be sitting here in my office. I'm just playing the devil's advocate and even though I may believe you're innocent the authorities may not. By the way, what time did you leave work last night?"

"Same as always, about five-thirty—quarter to six."

"Go straight home?"

"Yes."

"Stay home all night?"

"Yes. And yes, I was alone. I left for the office this morning around seven or seven-fifteen."

"Don't be so defensive. Remember, I'm on your side. Did you see Twyla after you left the coffee shop?"

"Sorry, can't help it. And no, I didn't see Twyla again after we left the coffee shop."

"It'll be interesting to see if you were the last person to be with Twyla before she disappeared."

"Yeah! Like someone else is going to come forward and admit to abducting or even killing her. All of this is beginning to have a familiar ring. First Penny, then Twyla."

"That may be the reason you're in law enforcements sights. You had a motive to eliminate Penny and a motive to eliminate the key witness against you in the murder case."

"Maybe Twyla will show up," I say but deep in my gut I know she won't or at least not for a while.

"Twyla's disappearance isn't all bad. In fact, it works in our favor. If she doesn't show up in time for the murder case, you're home free. No body, no motive, no conviction. Twyla's the only one who can prove the affair if you don't testify."

"What about her testimony before the grand jury? According to her testimony before the grand jury in the discovery the DA provided, she testified we were having an affair."

"Being sequestered from the proceedings is a double edged sword. We, of course, didn't get a chance to examine the witness but since we were not present at the grand jury proceedings and didn't have the opportunity to cross examine Twyla, the prosecution can't use her testimony at trial. It would be a violation of the Sixth Amendment."

"The Sixth Amendment?"

"Yes, the one that affords an accused a fair trial and the right to confront witnesses against him or her."

Bless all you framers of the constitution. "Do you think the DA will drop Penny's murder case if Twyla doesn't testify?"

"The DA may think he has enough other evidence to proceed with a second degree murder charge. I doubt he would just dismiss the case outright."

"I'm no lawyer, but I can't for the life of me see how they can connect me to Penny's disappearance. How do they know I was the last person to see her? In fact, how do they even know she's not still alive?"

"To answer your questions, they can't. That calls for speculation. Without strong circumstantial evidence such as blood splatters, DNA, evidence of a struggle, some kind of weapon with Penny's blood on it such as a knife or other object, the DA doesn't have much of a case. Unfortunately, since the DA convened a grand jury to make the charging decision, after they return an indictment, the DA is almost forced to proceed."

The cards continue to be stacked against me. I'm afraid to ask but I do anyway. "Do you think I'll be charged in Twyla's disappearance since I presumably was the last person she was seen with?"

Will's matter-or-fact answer does little to quell my fears. "Who knows? It's still too early to draw any conclusions. Since the authorities are convinced that you somehow did away with Penny they might draw the same conclusion with regard to Twyla. Since Twyla is the key witness in Penny's case they have motive. As far as means and opportunity, those elements can be inferred by the hour only you can account for and your respective physical builds. You're what six three or four and weigh about two forty and Twyla is about five seven and a hundred and thirty-five pounds?"

"Pretty close. But how could I have killed and disposed of Twyla's body and vehicle in an hour?"

"You'd have had plenty of time to kill Twyla and conceal the vehicle during the lunch break. In other words, hypothetically, you and Twyla could have left her vehicle at some other location and driven in your vehicle to your home ostensibly for lunch. Afterwards, you could have taken her to see the horses and killed her in the horse barn. Then after work you could have disposed of her body."

"Is that what *you* think?"

"No, but that may be the way the authorities will be looking at it in light of what happened to Penny."

"I never saw Twyla after we left the coffee shop—I swear."

"I believe you. The problem is once a suspect always a suspect. The similarities of the two disappearances and the common denominator make you the prime suspect."

I shake my head in disbelief, "How is it me having an affair translates into me being a killer?"

"It wouldn't have been if it had not involved both your wife and the other woman. When a suspect's house of cards begins to crumble and the wife finds out about the affair the suspect usually rushes to cover his indiscretions—in this case both women disappeared. It's a scenario used by investigators. Often the way it plays out is that the prime suspect actually does turn out to be the perp. I guess one could argue that Penny staged her disappearance to frame you and Twyla staged her disappearance to divert attention away from her and make you the fall guy."

"You don't think Twyla had Penny killed while we were in Cincinnati thereby establishing an alibi and is now afraid she'll be implicated in the plot do you? If Penny is dead, the hired killer may be caught and implicate Twyla. With her perceiving that the authorities are closing in she no doubt is desperate and feels the only way out is to flee with the fifty thousand I paid her."

"Her husband could have found out about the two of you having coffee together and in a heated argument killed her."

I think about that for a moment before I reply, "That's a possibility. However, Roy is a mouse and I don't think he would hurt a fly let alone kill his wife. Then again, you never know."

"We'll find out soon enough whether you'll be charged with anything. I have a feeling Debow will also be taking this one before the grand jury. If you're subpoenaed, we'll plead the Fifth."

"How about a polygraph?"

"Let's wait and see how this all plays out."

Being stunned is something I've grown accustomed to lately. When I read the article in the morning edition of the *Erie Chronicle*, I can't believe my eyes.

KEY WITNESS DISAPPEARS

According to reliable sources, the key witness in the prosecution of businessman Denton Ballard has vanished. Dr. Roy Marin, husband of Twyla Marin, former secretary at Azar Publishers, Inc., a company founded by Ballard, yesterday filed a missing person's report. Apparently Twyla Marin, a prosecution witness in the first degree murder case of Ballard, was seen in Ballard's company just prior to her disappearance.

Almost two months ago Ballard's wife, Penny, disappeared under suspicious circumstances and a first degree murder charge was filed against Ballard. For that case he was released on $100,000 bond.

When contacted, District Attorney Arthur Debow declined to comment on whether Ballard would be charged in the disappearance of Twyla Marin.

"At this stage, there's no evidence that she's the victim of foul play," he said. Ballard could not be reached for comment.

As if the front page story wasn't enough the editorial was even worse.

DISTORTED JUSTICE

Two months after businessman Denton Ballard was released on bond in the death of his wife, the key witness in his case also vanishes.

Where the bond is usually set in first degree murder cases at one million dollars or more, Ballard's bond was set at only one hundred thousand.

Curious why Ballard received favorable treatment from District Court Judge Madeline Stockton.

Even though Ballard was under a no contact order in a sexual assault/harassment case brought by the key witness against him he was seen having coffee with her just prior to her disappearance. Did he buy her off or did he off her?

In our opinion, Ballard shouldn't have been out on bond at all let alone on a one hundred thousand dollar bond. If he hadn't been released, authorities wouldn't be searching frantically for their key witness, the wife of a prominent local physician.

When I telephone Will, he says, "You beat me to the punch. I was just getting ready to call you."

"You read the morning edition of the *Chronicle?*"

"I did and wondered where the leak came from."

"From someone who wanted to sway public opinion obviously. Looks like I've now been tried and convicted without even having to go to court."

To add insult to injury, Bidwell filed a motion to have me held in contempt of court for violation of the no contact order. After Jill and I testify as to who contacted who, Bidwell's request is denied. Twyla's husband was present in court and had some choice words for the judge. "If you're not careful," Judge Weber warns, "I'll be holding *you* in contempt."

On the way out of the courtroom, the good doctor approaches me. "Ballard, you son-of-a-bitch! First you cause Penny's disappearance and now Twyla's. I hope your sorry ass rots in hell!" Will restrains me when I clinch my fist and step toward Roy. "Easy, partner," he says. "He's not worth it. Besides we have enough on our plate to last a lifetime."

As we drive back to Will's office, he says, "That was a side of you I hadn't seen before. You have a pretty short fuse."

"I inherited my temper from my father. During my teens and twenties, I had a terrible temper. I've pretty much learned to control it. Lately, I've become pretty edgy and harboring a lot of resentment."

"Your temper ever get you in trouble?"

"Oh yeah! I spent more time in the principal's office than I did in the classroom. I was a golden glove champion in the day but I also got my clock cleaned a few times. Sometime I'll tell you about some of the street fights I had in college and graduate school—over some pretty stupid stuff."

8

WIN SOME-LOSE SOME

THE ERIE CHRONICLE is not the only publication to crucify me and the electronic media is having a heyday with its negative coverage of both disappearances. The crusaders against domestic violence and sexual harassment in the workplace have targeted me as a blight on society. I'm their new poster child. They boycott my business and block my passage shouting obscenities on a constant basis. Without police intervention, I'd have already been burned at the stake. Not even the abortion clinics attracted that much attention.

"We'll file a motion for change of venue," Will says. "There's no way you can receive a fair trial in Boulder County. The coverage has been so massive and pervasive that I'm not sure you can receive a fair trial anywhere in Colorado."

Mob rule is suddenly a reality in my life. Even my attorney doesn't think I can get a fair trial. "So what's the alternative? Can the case be tried in another state?"

"I doubt that would occur. My guess is it would be transferred either to Pueblo County or El Paso County."

"What other motions will we file?"

"Motions for discovery and maybe suppression of statements. We need the transcript of the grand jury proceedings for starters and we may or may not want to suppress your statements to the sheriff's deputies prior to your having been given your *Miranda* warnings."

"When I spoke with the deputies I denied having had an affair with Twyla."

"You also told them Penny was upset with you because she thought you were having an affair with your secretary. And you admitted that Twyla had accompanied you to Cincinnati about the time of Penny's disappearance. Even if your statements are suppressed the latter statement can probably be proven through other witnesses such as Jill Caragon and Twyla's husband."

"And if I don't testify?"

"Then the affair can't come in. As I've said, only two people were aware of the affair—you and Twyla. And what Twyla told others including her testimony before the grand jury is hearsay and not admissible."

So, under the circumstances, I'm pretty sure I won't be testifying. However, for further clarification I ask, "And if I do testify?"

"You open the door so to speak. By testifying you were not responsible for Penny's disappearance you in essence would be conveying you had no motive. If you do take the stand, the other side has wide latitude in cross-examination. They can then delve into your affair with Twyla. Remember you'll be under oath and will have to tell the truth. If you lie, your testimony will be impeached and even worse you could be charged with perjury."

I feel myself slump in my chair when I realize the gravity of my situation. "So if I get on the stand and say I didn't have anything to do with Penny's disappearance and that's all I testify to, I can still be cross-examined about all kinds of other things?" "Precisely! Your affair with Twyla would only be the beginning. The prosecution can then explore motive, opportunity and means. When Debow gets through with you, you'll look like mincemeat. In other words, through you they can get in evidence things that would otherwise be inadmissible."

"What did you mean when you said we may or may not want to suppress my statements to Fuller and Whittaker?"

"We can get your denial of not having had anything to do with Penny's disappearance into evidence without you having to testify if we allow the statements to come in. Unfortunately, that means what you said about Penny's suspicions will also come in. The idea of an affair will then be planted firmly in the minds of the jury."

My head is reeling trying to sort through the intricacies of how to manipulate testimony to get in favorable testimony and keep out damaging evidence. "Isn't the tradeoff in our favor?"

"Actually Penny's suspicions might work *in your favor.*"

"You mean a reason she might want to leave me and stage her disappearance in such a way as to point the finger of suspicion in my direction?"

"That certainly appears to be the case. You said she was vindictive. What better way to even the score and tie a noose around your neck than make you appear to be the cause of her disappearance."

"Does that mean you're inclined or not inclined to file a motion to suppress statements?"

"Not! It's the only way I know to get your denial before the jury without subjecting you to cross-examination. Besides it's doubtful the judge would grant our motion since you were not 'in custody' at the time you made the statements."

"Any other motions?"

"Motion to allow introduction of your polygraph results into evidence and a motion excluding the statements Twyla made to third persons."

"I thought you said polygraph results were not admissible?"

"They're thought to be inadmissible but I think we have nothing to lose by seeking their admission. At least it makes the court aware you passed the polygraph as well as a press that is only too eager to print anything that's incriminating."

"Aren't statements made by Twyla hearsay?"

"They are but the prosecution may try to get them admitted under the unavailability of witness rule. As I previously stated, because Twyla was not subject to being cross-examined, they're inadmissible. For the prosecution to try to get the statements admitted in front of the jury would be just as devastating as the statements themselves. This way a prior ruling by the court prevents that from happening."

Now it's beginning to make sense. "What witnesses will Debow call?"

"They've endorsed Lance Whittaker, Madalyn Fuller, Twyla Marin, Dr. Roy Marin, Jill Caragon, Renee Stapleton and Caleb Bidwell."

"Caleb Bidwell? Why Caleb Bidwell?"

"They may try to get the sexual assault/harassment case before the jury. With Twyla out of the picture it has no relevance and even if she were to testify it has no relevance. I think if you testify they may want to use the settlement in that case to refute any notion that she's a suspect. In other words, to counter the alternative suspect theory. Also, if you testify and deny having had a motive to kill Penny and deny having had an affair with Twyla, they could use it in an attempt to impeach you. After all, why would you settle the case and not fight it if the case didn't have merit?"

Things are looking up. Maybe Twyla did *me* a favor by disappearing. "It doesn't sound like they have much of a case without the testimony of their star witness."

"That's a logical assumption. However, stranger things have happened. Trying to outguess a jury is next to impossible. Let's hope they don't convict on the basis of appearances or public opinion."

I shudder. That last remark triggers memories of the newspaper stories vilifying me along with the abuse, harassment and hate speech I've had to endure.

The motions hearing is short and sweet. Will has several members of the community testify that because of the massive and pervasive nature of the pretrial publicity they're convinced I'm guilty. Debow counters with several witnesses of his own who testify they're not persuaded one way or the other by the pretrial publicity. Judge Stockton rules in our favor and the case is transferred to Colorado Springs. Since discovery is required under Colorado law our motion for discovery is granted and all documents, reports and anything relative to our case including the transcript of the grand jury proceedings are ordered to be turned over to us.

Our motion to exclude Twyla's out of court statements are granted but the motion to admit the polygraph results is summarily denied.

"Three out of four ain't bad," I whisper to Will.

"Win some-lose some," Will whispers back.

As a last minute gesture, Debow requests that my bond be revoked since I'm a suspect in connection with the disappearance of the prosecution's key witness. "The defendant is a flight risk. In light of Ms. Marin's disappearance and him being the prime suspect," Debow argues, "and for the protection of the other witnesses, we request defendant's bond be revoked."

"Do you wish to be heard?" Judge Stockton asks and peers over her glasses at Will.

"We do, Your Honor." Will stands and moves to the podium. He leans his forearms against the incline and stares off into space for a moment and then dramatically looks back at Judge Stockton. "Judge," he begins. "How is it two disappearances transform my client into a criminal? In one case he's a prime suspect because he's the husband. In the other the husband is not the prime suspect. With no bodies the absence of both women is aptly described as *disappearances*. That means it's possible they may reappear. What evidence does the prosecution have that either one is the victim of foul play? Yet in the case now before you, Mr. Ballard is charged with first degree murder. In regard to the second disappearance no charges have been filed against anyone. The evidence is speculative at best that any crime has been committed in either of the two cases let alone that Mr. Ballard is the perpetrator.

"Mr. Ballard has no criminal record and no blood on his hands." Will looks back at me for a moment. "Despite his conviction by the press and maybe in public opinion, the status of his case remains the same. The proof is not evident and the presumption is not great. Therefore under the law he is entitled to be released on bond. To incarcerate him pending a determination of guilt is to prejudge him and punish him by depriving him of his freedom. If the bond is revoked and he is incarcerated, we request an expedited trial date."

Debow jumps up. "Your Honor, we object to an expedited trial date! The prosecution is still without its star witness and we request a reasonable amount of time for her to…return."

"Mr. Debow," Judge Stockton says and removes her glasses, "you can't have your cake and eat it too. On the one hand you infer that *maybe* Mr. Ballard caused your key witness's disappearance and *maybe* something even more sinister and now you're telling the court that you need time to make sure of her availability or unavailability. You can't have it both ways."

Debow shrugs and shrinks back into his chair.

Judge Stockton rubs her forehead for several moments and finally says, "The court has given your arguments much consideration. In light of all the circumstances, the court can't risk harm befalling the other prosecution witnesses nor the possibility that facing serious charges in two cases the defendant might flee and disappear like the victim and key witness in the instant case."

Looking directly at me, Judge Stockton says, "The court is torn between allowing you to remain on bail on the one hand and protecting society from a potential risk on the other. I have to consider your rights and weigh them against the rights of society. In doing so, I have no recourse but to revoke your bond."

I nod. "I understand," I say even though I really don't. "What about the presumption of innocence?" I lean over and whisper to Will.

Judge Stockton continues, "With regard to the defendant's request for an expedited trial and considering the special circumstances connected with this case, the court will grant the motion for speedy trial and place the case on a fast track." She motions for her clerk to bring her the court's calendar. After scanning the pages, Judge Stockton says, "We can set this for a two week trial commencing November sixth. That's ninety days from today's date."

"That would be agreeable to the defense, Will says.

"The prosecution will be available on that date depending on the availability of our key witness," Debow says.

Shaking her head and leaning forward on her forearms, the judge glares down at Debow and says, "Mr. Debow, apparently I have not made myself clear. Available or not and ready or not trial in this case will commence promptly at eight a.m. on November the sixth, twenty seventeen." The judge closes the cover of her calendar and passes it back to her clerk signaling the end of discussion, "Do I make myself clear?"

"Yes, Your Honor," Debow says meekly.

"Very well, then," Judge Stockton says, "court will stand adjourned until that date. Mr. Ballard will be remanded into the custody of the sheriff of Boulder County pending trial."

I'm handcuffed and transported to the Boulder County jail where I'm processed. I trade my civilian attire for jail garb and all my personal belongings are confiscated before I'm placed in a dark, dingy cell. I'm severely depressed and feel the criminal justice system that was designed to protect human dignity and ensure due process is a farce. In my case there is no presumption of innocence only a presumption of guilt—a presumption that I must overcome in order to have my freedom restored.

My first night in the slammer is unnerving. I toss and turn on the narrow cot and finally fall into deep slumber just before I'm awakened by one of the jailers. "Chow in fifteen," he says. I sit on the edge of my cot and rub sleep from my eyes. My whole body feels like a marauding herd of elephants trampled me. When I stand my back spasms and I'm not sure my legs will support me. I groan in pain and despair.

When the cells are opened and the inmates line up, I'm positioned behind some pretty unsavory characters. *Wouldn't want to meet any of these guys in a dark alley!* This bunch must be regulars as they hang together. I'm ostracized and they treat me as though I have leprosy. *Just as well!* I prefer to be alone and not engage in conversation.

Back in my cell after breakfast, I mentally run through what Will said as I was being led from the courtroom. "The test of a man is how he reacts when he's under fire and things look bleak."

The next day when Will visits me he brings with him the morning edition of the *Erie Chronicle*. He hands it to me and says, "We made the front page again."

I flinch when I open the front page and see a large colored photo of me being led from the courtroom in handcuffs by two uniformed deputies. The caption under the photograph reads: "Pictured above being led from the courtroom of the Boulder County Courthouse in handcuffs is businessman Denton Ballard who has been charged with first degree murder in the disappearance of his wife, Penny."

The headline reads:

BOND FOR ALLEGED KILLER REVOKED

I'm not sure I want to read the lengthy story that follows but my curiosity gets the better of me. My hands shake so violently that I have to place the paper on my lap in order to read it.

Upon motion of district attorney, Arthur Debow, the bond of Erie businessman Denton Ballard was revoked. Judge Madeline Stockton, who originally granted Ballard the highly controversial $100,000 bond, said she reversed herself because Ballard was a flight risk and may have been involved in the disappearance of still another woman—the key witness in the murder prosecution.

According to sources close to the *Erie Chronicle*, Ballard is also the prime suspect in the disappearance of Twyla Marin, a former secretary of Ballard and the key witness against him in the murder prosecution of his wife.

At yesterday's motions hearing, a defense motion to have the case transferred to another venue because of "massive and pervasive pretrial publicity" was granted. Judge Stockton transferred the case to El Paso County and granted defense counsel Willard Crowley's motion to expedite the trial date. The case is set for a two week trial commencing on November 6.

Another of defense's motions, production of grand jury minutes, reports, list of prosecution witnesses and evidence to be presented at trial, was also granted along with their request to exclude out of court statements made by Twyla Marin. Defense's motion to allow Ballard's favorable polygraph results to be admitted in evidence however was denied.

When asked what effect the possibility that Ballard might be charged in still another disappearance case would have on the current prosecution, Crowley told the *Erie Chronicle*, "None. Just another case of justice gone awry and a waste of taxpayer money."

When interviewed by the *Erie Chronicle*, district attorney Arthur Debow said he wasn't sure if he would file criminal charges against Ballard in connection with the disappearance of Twyla Marin and would probably take the case before the grand jury as he had in the disappearance of Penny Ballard. Twyla Marin was reported missing by her husband, Dr. Roy Marin, on July 23 after being seen with Ballard at a coffee shop in the forenoon. Penny Ballard was reported missing on March 13. To date there is no word as to the whereabouts of either woman.

I shake my head in disbelief and look up. When I start to hand the newspaper back to Will, he says, "You also need to read the editorial."

"What's it say?" I ask and cringe at the prospect of still another blistering attack on me.

Will takes the paper and turns to the editorial page. Folding it so only the scathing editorial is exposed, he hands it back to me. I read the following:

BETTER LATE THAN NEVER

Judge Madeline Stockton finally got it right in revoking the bond of Denton Ballard charged in the presumed death of his wife Penny. Had the good judge done it right the first time she possibly could have prevented the mysterious disappearance of Twyla Marin, a former secretary of Ballard and the key witness in his murder prosecution.

The *Erie Chronicle* was critical of Judge Stockton's setting of bail shortly after Ballard's arrest. A $100,000 bond seemed hardly appropriate and that sentiment was shared by the many letters to the editor who denounced Judge Stockton's even allowing Ballard to be released on bail.

Our hearts go out to Twyla Marin's husband Dr. Roy Marin who has to bear the brunt of Judge Stockton's initial ill-advised bond setting.

Feeling more helpless than ever, I ask Will, "When will this nightmare end?"

"After the jury hears the evidence!" Will replies. "Even though the evidence or lack thereof speaks for itself, you may want to take another polygraph?"

"Absolutely. I'll pass it just like I did in Penny's case."

"Since you haven't been charged, passing a poly in Twyla's case might ward off another frivolous prosecution."

I nod but a foreboding gloom assaults me. "What good is passing the polygraph if it can't be used in court?" I ask and bite my lip.

This time Will relents and allows the polygrapher employed by the sheriff's office to administer the polygraph. "The results can't be used anyway and maybe if it's administered by one of their own, they may be more inclined to accept the results."

I take and pass still another polygraph. Will, armed with the results, attempts to persuade Debow not to file charges in connection with Twyla's disappearance.

As the trial date approaches in connection with Penny's disappearance, I'm given the bad news that the grand jury has returned an indictment charging me with first degree murder and obstruction of justice in Twyla's case. I seem to lose every time the cards are dealt.

The prosecution's motion to join both cases is denied and so is their alternate motion to be able to refer to the case involving Twyla in Penny's case. In making her ruling, Judge Stockton ruled that, "The probative value of what the prosecution seeks is outweighed by the prejudicial effect."

"The timing of the filing of the second case is hardly coincidental," Will says. "Since there is no statute of limitations for murder, they could have waited until after the resolution of Penny's case. I can only think they did it for the psychological effect."

"I thought prosecutors took an oath to seek justice not convictions," I say.

"Sometimes ego gets in the way of good judgment," Will says. "Debow runs every four years for public office and he seems to be pandering to the public in light of the public sentiment spawned by an unscrupulous press."

"An unscrupulous press coupled with an over-zealous prosecutor is a bad combination!"

"Couldn't have said it better myself," Will laughs. "Isn't that what I stated to Judge Stockton when I requested the change of venue?"

"It is," I say. "Thought if you could use it, I could as well."

"Smart boy!"

"Wish Judge Stockton hadn't been swayed by public opinion and her desire to cater to a bias press."

"Win some, lose some," Will says. "We've made significant progress and head into trial with the law and the facts in our favor."

9

PEOPLE v. BALLARD I

I HAVE A calendar in my cell and mark off the days remaining until trial. I appreciate more and more the plight of the condemned. I've been told jail life is a piece of cake compared to prison life. "What are the chances I'll receive the death penalty?" I ask Will.

"With no body and no motive there's no evidence of premeditation and deliberation. That means that the jury at worst could come back with second degree murder or manslaughter. Neither are considered capital offenses and therefore the possible sentence would be a prison term."

"But I haven't been charged with either second degree murder or manslaughter."

"They're considered *lesser included* offenses of first degree murder and therefore don't need to be charged. The jury will be provided a verdict form that necessarily lists all three possibilities: first degree murder, second degree murder or manslaughter. If the jury finds you guilty, they have the opportunity to choose and mark the charge on the form that best fits their assessment of your guilt. However, they can choose only one from the list."

I give Will a blank stare.

"In other words, if the jury finds you caused Penny's death but didn't do so intentionally, they could find you guilty of one of the lesser included offenses depending on the circumstances."

I nod. "What are the penalties for second degree murder and manslaughter?"

"Second degree murder carries a possible penalty of eight to twelve years in the Colorado State Penitentiary unless the killing was performed upon a sudden heat of passion caused by a serious and highly provoking act in which case it would be four to eight years. Manslaughter carries a possible penalty of two to four years."

"If I'm convicted of first degree murder I could receive life imprisonment or death. If Twyla mysteriously reappears and testifies as to our affair, what's the likelihood I'd be convicted of first degree murder?"

"Even with Twyla's testimony, with no proof of Penny's death you shouldn't be convicted of either murder or manslaughter. On the off chance you were convicted of first degree murder, it's highly unlikely you'd receive the death penalty."

"Life imprisonment would probably be worse than the death penalty."

"There's always the possibility Penny may reappear on the scene in which case your conviction would be set aside and you'd be a free man."

"Not much consolation!"

"Better than the alternative!"

The next time we meet we discuss potential witnesses. We start first with the prosecution witnesses in the order in which they were endorsed. Leading the list is a new addition, Fran Wilson, the 911 operator I spoke to when I first discovered Penny missing.

"Can they do that?" I ask.

"Do what?" Will replies.

"Add witnesses."

"Apparently when the prosecution was preparing for trial they discovered they had inadvertently left Fran off the list. Since her report appears in the discovery we can't claim surprise. They of course can't call witnesses they haven't endorsed. Neither can we. To object to her late endorsement would be a waste of everyone's time. Besides, we need her as a witness and you'll notice we endorsed her as one of our witnesses."

Will had a copy of the discovery duplicated for me when he first received it. I've gone over it many times and find Twyla's report to be the most damaging. I'm also concerned about her husband's proposed testimony. Will has convinced me that anything Twyla told her husband would be considered hearsay and inadmissible in court. Since we are taking the witnesses in the order of their endorsement I'm reluctant to interrupt the flow.

Will writes the name Fran Wilson on the white board in his office. "I'm hoping we won't have to call Fran as our witness and can get everything in on cross-examination," Will says.

When he looks at me I frown. He further explains, "I anticipate Fran will be the first witness the prosecution will call. By an effective cross-examination, we can make her our witness and get the jury thinking our way right from the start."

"Makes sense," I say.

"By instigating the call to 911 and not disturbing the evidence, you have demonstrated a concern for your wife that all of us can relate to. You could have just as easily staged a break-in if you had done away with your wife and bolstered a more believable scenario than she just disappeared. If you had had a hand in her disappearance, you'd have removed all the personal items and maybe disposed of her SUV and made it look like a tornado hit the place. Instead, you called 911 and thereby made yourself the prime suspect in her disappearance." Will looks at me and raises his brows.

"I was thinking about all of the unfavorable evidence and how easily some of it can be slanted in my favor," I say.

"Be prepared. Debow will zero in on the improbability of someone just disappearing from the face of the earth and leaving their ID and SUV behind, that is unless they met with some type of disaster."

"I'm inclined to believe she had someone helping her or else was abducted."

"If someone was helping her, it's unlikely she'd have left things like her driver's license, credit cards and personal items behind."

"She had the one hundred thousand dollars from our home safe."

"Still doesn't explain why she didn't take her driver's license."

"Obviously to make it appear I had a hand in her disappearance."

"As I've been saying, she did a great job!"

The names of Lance Whittaker and Madeline Fuller are next to be listed on the white board. "Convinced you're guilty, Whittaker and Fuller will slant the evidence in the prosecution's favor. It's our job to dilute their testimony and convince the jury that in their haste to solve the murder mystery, if such there be, they zeroed in on the most vulnerable target and overlooked the possibility of an alternate suspect. Unfortunately for us we can't get in your polygraph results; unfortunately for them they can't get into evidence your affair with Twyla unless she testifies or we open the door."

Will writes the name of Twyla Marin on the white board and crosses it off. He then lists the names of Dr. Roy Marin, Jill Caragon, Renee Stapleton and Caleb Bidwell on the white board.

"These are iffy witnesses," Will says. "Depending on your testimony and whether Twyla shows up for trial the only one to make an appearance will be Jill Caragon and she'll be our witness."

"But I won't be testifying," I say.

"Neither will any of the other witnesses. I have a feeling Debow will be saving them for rebuttal to counter your testimony. If you don't testify he won't have anything to counter. If they have anything of a probative nature to testify to they will be precluded from doing so. The only one of the group we have endorsed and will be calling is Jill Caragon as I've already stated."

"She along with Penny's sister, Kay, will be our only witnesses. Correct?"

"Not necessarily. We have also endorsed Penny's mother, Gladys Gerard. She can testify as to Penny's disappearance when Penny was in high school. That will demonstrate to the jury Penny's propensity to absent herself when things don't go her way and a way of expressing her displeasure."

"Kay could also testify to that."

"Kay will be testifying as to having been with you and Penny when you won Kamanda for Penny and attached your fraternity pin to Kamanda and presented Kamanda to Penny. Jill was there when you opened up the package from Penny upon your return from Cincinnati that contained Kamanda with the fraternity pin still attached."

"How come we didn't endorse Kamanda?"

"Will laughs. "Glad to see you still have a sense of humor. Kamanda is our ace in the hole and our key to an acquittal. Kay can also testify as to Penny's engagement and wedding rings being found in Kamanda's secret pocket."

"I see you also endorsed Penny's father."

"Harry Gerard was endorsed in case we need him. Depending on the prosecution's case-in-chief, he may or may not be called."

"What does he add?"

"He can testify as to the safe being emptied. Ordinarily, you'd be testifying to that. With the decision not to call you, the only way we can get that evidence before the jury is through your father-in-law."

"When you say depending on what the prosecution presents, doesn't the evidence about the empty safe work in our favor?"

"Maybe yes and maybe no. The prosecution could argue your staged the scene to look like a robbery and an abduction."

"If that was the case, I did a pretty poor job."

"I've prosecuted and defended a lot of cases in my career. This is the first where almost all the evidence could be viewed both ways—to absolve you and to incriminate you. It all boils down to what scenario is the most believable. We are handicapped by not being able to call you as a witness. The jury expects that the innocent will speak in their own behalf and the guilty will plead the Fifth."

"That places me in one hell of a fix. If I testify I establish motive and if I don't my silence is construed as guilt. Either way, I seal my own fate."

"It's not over 'till it's over."

It's the eve of trial and still no Penny or Twyla. Will has arranged for me to be free of my cuffs and dressed in civilian attire when I appear in court. Both my parents and Penny's visit me in jail. Both give me the courage to persevere. Penny's sisters, Kay and Amanda and their husbands won't be arriving until mid-morning on Monday.

According to Will, with the death penalty on the table, jury selection could take the better part of the week. Because of the sequestration of witnesses rule being in effect, potential witnesses cannot remain in the courtroom once the jury has been selected. Otherwise they will be precluded from testifying.

When I arrive in the courtroom it's packed. Most are prospective jurors and the press. My parents and in-laws arrived early enough to be seated in the front row. They give me an abbreviated wave and smile. Even though I'm stressed and embarrassed, I return their smiles. I'm led by two deputies to the defense table where Will is seated along with one of the associates from his firm, a female attorney by the name of Jessica Sanders. Jessica moves over when I arrive and I'm placed between the two of them.

At the prosecution's table is Debow, his assistant, Darrell Reader, a burly man in his late fifties, and Fuller who is designated as an advisory witness and therefore allowed to remain in the courtroom while other witnesses testify.

I'm not as nervous as I thought I'd be. With both my parents and Penny's pulling for me, I no longer feel alone in a sea of discontent.

When Judge Stockton enters the courtroom, the bailiff orders us to stand. He calls the court to order.

"Please be seated," Judge Stockton orders as she takes her place at the bench. We all oblige and we're soon immersed in the jury selection process. Twelve names are called and after the judge asks the obligatory questions, Debow and Will attempt to determine who would be ideal jurors to sit in judgement in my case.

Will wants sympathetic jurors and Debow wants vigilantes. Those who state that under no set of circumstances could they impose the death penalty are excused by the court. So much for sympathetic jurors. None indicate they read anything about the case or have made up their minds as to my guilt or innocence. *The change of venue accomplished its intended goal.* All said they would be fair and impartial. Some were excused by Debow and some by Will. Their replacements are acceptable to both sides. As unlikely as it seems, we have a jury by the end of the first day. It's an even split between male and female. Several are in their twenties and the rest are forty or older. Only one is retired.

The jury is sworn in and soon excused for the day. They are ordered to return at 8:00 a.m. on Tuesday. Those who are not selected are told to report to the jury commissioner for further jury duty. Judge Stockton instructs the attorneys on both sides to be ready for opening statements when court convenes the following day.

When I have been placed back in the holding cell, Will is allowed to confer with me in private.

"What do you think of our jury?" I ask Will.

"I didn't detect any hostility toward you when the judge informed the jury of the nature of the charges," he replies.

"Some ceased to look at me and avoided eye contact when Stockton stated one of the charges was first degree murder."

"That's a natural tendency. Even though the jurors denied aspiring to the belief that *Where there's smoke, there's fire!* that doesn't mean that thought won't creep into their minds."

"Let's hope it's short-lived."

"Remember, they'll hear the prosecution's side of the case first. That's why cross-examination is so important. Once they make up their minds they can't easily be persuaded otherwise."

"You pretty much covered that with several prospective jurors when you asked them to listen to all the evidence before making up their minds."

"They know how to slant their answers to fit their desire to serve or not serve. Some may do it deliberately and some inadvertently. The challenge is to determine who is posturing and who isn't."

"The real test I guess is what verdict they return."

"The cases you think you win you don't and the cases you don't think you'll win you do. So, go figure."

When I'm *ushered* to my seat at the defendant's table, Will and Jessica are already there. My parents, Amanda and her husband Eric, are seated in what will become their regular spot in the front row of the spectator's section. Penny's parents and sister Kay are not in attendance since they may be called as witnesses. They are sequestered so that their recollection will not be tainted by the testimony of other witnesses.

Will stands and shakes my hand and asks how I'm doing. However, we don't spend much time chatting as he immediately turns his attention back to concentrating on his opening statement. I notice Jessica is poised to take notes on Debow's opening.

When Will looks up from his notepad, I ask, "Will you be giving our opening statement following Debow's or will you wait until the start of our case-in-chief?"

"Depends on how effective Debow's opening is. Probably do as I usually do—wait until it's our turn to put on our case. Don't want to reveal our battle plan until we have to. Otherwise Debow will have time to counter it in the prosecution's case-in-chief."

"Makes sense," I say and hope with all my heart Will knows what he's doing. *Just pray he's as good as everyone says he is!*

Debow is sporting his infamous banker's suit. Unlike the last time he was in court, he is clean shaven.

"Wants to look more like a law school prof," Will says. Colorado Springs is a little more conservative than Boulder."

"Most places are," I say. "Maybe we should have kept the case in Boulder."

"If you hadn't already been tried and convicted by the press we probably wouldn't have asked for a change of venue."

"Sorry to keep you waiting," Judge Stockton says as she enters and takes her place on the bench. "Had an urgent matter to attend to in chambers." She then asks if we're ready to proceed. When both sides indicate they are, she instructs the bailiff to usher in the jury.

The jurors seem friendly enough. The youngest juror, Louise Wilkinson, flashes me a smile. "They don't look like they've been scared off by the charges," I whisper to Will.

"That's a good sign," Will whispers back.

The prosecution may now make their opening statement," Judge Stockton says and looks in Debow's direction.

"Thank you, Your Honor," Debow says and struts to the podium. "Debow's way of disguising stage fright," Will whispers referring to Debow's swagger.

"Ladies and gentlemen," Debow begins, "opening statements are not evidence. They are nothing more than the revelation in outline fashion of what each side expects the evidence will show.

"On March eighteenth of this year the 911 dispatcher, Fran Wilson, received a call from someone identifying himself as Denton Ballard. He claimed that upon returning from a business trip to Cincinnati he took a cab home because his wife, Penny, the victim in this case, failed to pick him up. He claimed that when he entered the house he found his wife's purse, wallet and car keys on the kitchen countertop. Her SUV was in the garage and she was nowhere to be found.

"Boulder sheriff's deputies, Gretchen Fuller and Lance Whittaker were dispatched to the scene. They were met by Denton Ballard, the defendant in this case. When questioned as to why he reported his wife missing, he claimed the last time he saw her was on March fourteenth when she drove him to the airport. During the interview, when asked if he had an argument with his wife before his departure, the defendant stated yes. He said that she was upset with him for taking one of the secretaries from his firm with him to Cincinnati. He also claimed he talked to his wife by telephone the night before his return to Erie. However, when investigators obtained telephone records for both the landline and his wife's cellphone, no records were found to indicate that such a call was made.

"The evidence will show that when Deputies Fuller and Whittaker conducted a search of defendant's home they found no sign of any unlawful entry. When questioned about his wife's mysterious disappearance, defendant denied having any knowledge of her whereabouts. To date, there has been no contact from the victim and no body has turned up.

"If the evidence produced at trial is as the prosecution anticipates, we will have no hesitancy whatsoever at the end of the case in asking you to return guilty verdicts on all counts."

I'm devastated once again at the accusation that I had something to do with Penny's disappearance. I watch several jurors look at me and raise their brows. Will follows my gaze and comments, "Looks like the jury is underwhelmed at the prosecution's presentation."

"Mr. Crowley," Judge Stockton says, "will the defense be making its opening statement now or at the beginning of defendant's case-in-chief?"

"Your Honor, the defense will reserve its opening statement."

"Very well. Mr. Debow you may call your first witness."

Debow calls Fran Wilson to the stand, and after she is sworn in, she testifies as outlined in Debow's opening statement. At the conclusion of Wilson's testimony, Debow turns and gives Will a smirk. I interpret that as a challenge. It's Will's turn to cross-examine and when Will stands and whispers to me, "Hold the fort." That little gesture from Will give me confidence that justice will prevail.

"Ms. Wilson you've been a 911 dispatcher for Boulder County for how many years?"

"Next month will be the start of my fourteenth year."

"Fourteen years," Will says and looks at the jury. "During your tenure, I imagine you've spoken with a lot of frantic people."

Wilson smiles, "All the time."

"On a scale of one to ten, ten being the highest, how would you rate the call from Mr. Ballard?"

"Easily a ten," Wilson replies without hesitation.

"Easily a ten," Will repeats Wilson's response and glances at the jurors. "Now, drawing on your experience at having dealt with emergency calls for fourteen years, did it appear he was genuinely concerned about his wife's disappearance?"

Again no hesitation, "Absolutely!"

"In other words, you didn't think it was contrived?"

"No, not in the least."

"Did he tell you he looked all over for his wife and even saddled his horse and combed the hundred and sixty acres surrounding their home in search of her?"

"Yes."

"What happened when you told him that it was not common to become alarmed until seventy-two hours had passed?"

"He said his wife had left her wallet with her driver's license and credit cards behind and had left no note as was her usual custom when she left home. He also said he checked the garage and found both of their vehicles parked inside. He said he called several of her friends but no one had seen her and assumed she had travelled to Cincinnati with him."

"Did you ask him when he *saw* her last?"

"Yes, he said Wednesday the day he left for Cincinnati when she dropped him off at the airport."

"Did you ask when he last *spoke* to her?"

"Yes, he said the night before he was to return to Erie."

"Is it usual for you to notify the sheriff's department when you receive a missing person's report?"

"Yes."

"Even if the person hasn't been missing for seventy-two hours?"

"Yes."

I suspect that last question was for the jury to hammer home how concerned Wilson was to have passed the missing person's report on to the S.O. before the seventy-two hour wait period had elapsed.

"No further questions, Your Honor."

The next witness called by Debow is Gretchen Fuller. She's obviously convinced I'm guilty and wants the jury to feel the same. It's with disdain that she identifies me in court. *What the hell did I do to ruffle her feathers?*

Will's cross-examination is most effective. I can see how he earned the Perry Mason moniker.

"Why didn't you and Deputy Whittaker consider Mr. Ballard's report worthy of being labeled a *missing person's report?*"

"His wife left behind her SUV, car keys, cellphone and purse containing her wallet with her driver's license, credit cards and cash."

Examining his notes, Will asks, "Didn't you tell Mr. Ballard it was because she hadn't been missing for seventy-two hours?"

"That, too."

"And didn't Mr. Ballard say he wanted the FBI involved immediately and not wait for seventy-two hours?"

"Yes. We weren't certain yet whether or not Mrs. Ballard would return."

"Deputy Whittaker, by taking no action and not considering the alternative, didn't you consider valuable evidence could be lost?"

"As I said, we weren't convinced Mrs. Ballard would not be returning."

"If she were abducted the delay would give the abductor time to distance himself or herself far from the scene and out of your jurisdiction, would it not?"

"Possibly."

"Didn't you consider that?"

"Not at the time."

"Is that because you found no evidence of foul play?"

"Partially."

"At what point did you consider Mr. Ballard a suspect?"

"Right from the beginning."

"Right from the beginning? If that were the case then why didn't you advise him of his rights before you questioned him?"

"We did later."

"Later? Was that at the second interview?"

"Yes."

"Shouldn't he have been advised of his *Miranda* rights immediately upon questioning?"

"At first we were just trying to gather information."

"I see. Who initiated the second interview?"

"He did."

"Didn't it seem odd that a suspect would initiate not only one but two interviews?"

"Not necessarily."

"Isn't it true that you zeroed in on Mr. Ballard and spent the bulk of your time building a case against him instead of considering other alternatives?"

"Only because we found no evidence that anyone else was involved. We're obligated to follow the evidence." Fuller says and sounds like she's becoming unraveled.

Will presses on. "Didn't you consider the possibility that Mrs. Ballard staged her own disappearance out of spite and a way to punish her husband for his perceived infidelity?"

"We discounted that."

"Is that because of the personal items she left behind?"

"Pretty much."

"If Mr. Ballard were trying to make it appear that her disappearance was an abduction incident to a robbery or burglary, wouldn't he have staged the scene to make it appear so?"

"I suppose so."

"And if he wanted to make it appear his wife ran off with another man, for example, wouldn't he have gotten rid of all her personal belongings?"

"Possibly."

"To this date, you don't know for certain whether Penny Ballard is alive or dead, do you?"

"No."

"Is that because you've not found either her or her body?"

"Yes."

"In your direct testimony you claim phone records show no call from Penny to Mr. Ballard the night before Mr. Ballard's return from Cincinnati. Are you referring to no calls having been made from Penny's cellphone or the home phone?"

"Yes."

"If Penny called Mr. Ballard from a phone that was neither her cellphone nor the home phone, wouldn't that indicate that she called from some unknown phone?"

"Yes."

"Did you in your investigation identify the number from where the call had originated?"

"No."

"Didn't you think that was rather important since it might indicate where she was or where she had gone or who she was with?"

"Possibly."

"Just one more question." Will checks his notes. "When you asked Mr. Ballard whether he made the trip to Cincinnati alone and he told you his secretary accompanied him didn't he also explain why?"

"He said he was making a presentation at one of the sessions at the convention he was attending and she helped him with the power points."

"Did he explain that he was inept with electronics and needed her assistance?"

"Yes, he did."

"Thank you, Deputy Fuller. No further questions, Your Honor."

Will's cross-examination of Deputy Whittaker was just as impressive.

"Deputy Whittaker, on direct examination, you testified that the Boulder S.O. followed all leads."

"Correct. Our protocol is to leave no stone unturned."

"Un-huh. And did you contact Mrs. Ballard's parents to see if Mrs. Ballard was vindictive and had the propensity to run away from home when things didn't go her way?"

"Not that I'm aware."

"Don't investigators share information?"

"Of course."

"Then you'd had been aware if someone from the S.O. had contacted family members to see if maybe they knew the whereabouts of Mr. Ballard's wife or if she was in the habit of just disappearing."

"Is that a question?"

"Yes."

"No, no one told me they had spoken to family members other than Mr. Ballard."

"On direct, you also testified that you had determined Mr. Ballard was the last person to see his wife. Did you have reference to her having driven him to the airport?"

"Yes."

"That was on a Wednesday when Mr. Ballard left for Cincinnati?"

"Yes."

"Can you refute that?"

"No."

"Wasn't that five days before Mr. Ballard's return from Cincinnati?"

"Approximately."

"A lot of things could have happened while he was away?"

"Of course."

"And you checked to see what time Mr. Ballard's flight arrived at DIA?"

"Yes."

"How much time elapsed from the time he landed at DIA, claimed his luggage, returned home and called 911?"

"Approximately an hour and a half."

"Are you saying she disappeared during that hour and a half?"

"In checking with a neighbor Mrs. Ballard hadn't been home for several days and was thought to have travelled with Mr. Ballard to Cincinnati."

"You're not suggesting Mr. Ballard killed his wife when she dropped him off at the airport, are you?"

"That's a possibility."

Will looks at the jury then back at Whittaker. "Deputy Whittaker, did you check to see if anyone saw anything unusual happen at the airport around the time Mrs. Ballard would have dropped her husband off?"

"We did."

"And...?"

"None of the ones we interviewed saw anything unusual happen."

"And you obtained a copy of the passenger list for the flight to Cincinnati and Mr. Ballard's name was on it?"

"Yes."

"So when you testified under oath that Mr. Ballard was the last to see his wife, you don't really know that to be a fact, do you?"

I watch Whittaker give Will a blank stare and shrug.

"In other words, Deputy Whittaker, the fact that neither you nor any of the other investigators interviewed anyone who claims to have seen Mrs. Ballard doesn't necessarily mean Mr. Ballard was the last person to see his wife, does it?"

"I guess not."

"To be candid, Deputy Whittaker, it's the practice of your department and most police agencies to zero in on a close family member when there's a disappearance?"

"True."

"You zeroed in on Mr. Ballard and spent the better part of the last five or six months building a case against him. Is that not true?"

"That's where the evidence led us so I suppose you could say that."

"And if Mr. Ballard is not the cause of his wife's disappearance, you have squandered the opportunity to find out what really happened to Mrs. Ballard. Is that not true as well?"

Whittaker is having trouble disguising his disdain for Will. When Whittaker doesn't respond, Judge Stockton demands, "Please answer the question!"

Whittaker looks up at the judge and then back at Will. With no other alternative he finally answers. "I guess you could say that."

"Did you check to see if Mrs. Ballard had a life insurance policy?"

"Yes. That was one of the first things we did."

"Why did you do that?"

"To see if Mr. Ballard had a motive to kill his wife."

"Now tell the jury who the beneficiary of that policy was."

"The beneficiaries were Mrs. Ballard's twin sisters, Kay and Amanda."

"Mr. Ballard then wasn't the beneficiary of his wife's life insurance policy, was he?"

"No."

"When you and Deputy Fuller interviewed Mr. Ballard and he denied having anything to do with his wife's disappearance did he also tell the two of you that he loved his wife and would never do anything to harm her?"

"Yes."

Apparently Will is satisfied with Whittaker's responses. "No further questions, Your Honor," he says and sits down.

"Any other witnesses?" Judge Stockton asks Debow.

"May we have a minute?" Debow asks. The judge nods and Debow then confers with the two others seated at his table. Minutes tick by as we wait. Finally Debow says, "The prosecution rests."

Debow barely gets the words out before Will is on his feet. "We have a motion," Will says.

The judge holds up a hand, "Stay where you are, Mr. Crowley. It's late and we've already gone into the dinner hour. The court will recess until eight o'clock tomorrow morning at which time we will address your motion *in camera*." Judge Stockton then turns her attention toward the jury. "You are instructed to assemble in the jury room at nine a.m. tomorrow morning. You are now excused. You are instructed not to discuss this case with anyone or among yourselves or watch any newscasts concerning the case." Then turning to the rest of us, she says, "Everyone else will remain in the courtroom until the jury has departed."

Will leans over and whispers to me as the jury is ushered out by the bailiff. "It's obvious Debow is holding back their remaining witnesses until after you testify in the hopes you'll testify you had nothing to do with Penny's disappearance. That would open the door for them to bring in the affair and their most damaging evidence."

I whisper back, "Are we still going to rely on the presumption of innocence and not have me testify?"

"Yes." Will glances over at the prosecution's table where Debow's lackeys are gathering up the documents strewn about. "But they don't know that yet. It appears to me they think they have a slam-dunk case," Will says as he neatly stacks his files preparing to leave for the day. "There's a time to speak and a time to remain silent. Right now there's no evidence you had a motive to kill Penny, no body and no evidence she's not still alive."

I smile at the irony. "Looking good, huh?"

"It is what it is."

It's only the third day of trial and we're already presenting our case. We have Jill, Penny's parents and sister Kay, waiting in a witness room adjacent to the courtroom. Will met with them last night and he tells me they are primed. "We ran through a rehearsal and I put them through questions on direct and Jessica role-played Debow on cross."

Once we're assembled and before the jury is brought in, Judge Stockton looks over at Will, "You may present your motion, Mr. Crowley."

"Your Honor," Will begins, "the defense makes a motion for judgment of acquittal on the grounds that the evidence is lacking and when considered in the light most favorable to the people is insufficient to sustain a conviction and the case should not be submitted to the jury but instead dismissed."

Debow is instantly on his feet apparently ready to oppose the motion. Before he can say anything, Judge Stockton motions for him to sit. She says, "Mr. Crowley, the trial court must give the prosecution the benefit of every reasonable inference which might be fairly drawn from the evidence. The substantial evidence test must be applied which affords the same status to circumstantial evidence as to direct evidence. Therefore I have no recourse but to deny your motion." Then to the bailiff she says, "You may bring in the jury."

While we wait for the jury, I say to Will, "Who bought her off?"

"When Judge Stockton revoked your bond thus incarcerating you before you'd even been convicted was a signal that she believed you were somehow involved in Penny's disappearance. She painted herself into a corner and to save face she has placed the onus squarely on the jury in the event you are acquitted. With all the adverse public sentiment stacked against you she's afraid to incur public disfavor by granting the motion."

"I thought judges were supposed to be fair and impartial and not swayed by public opinion."

"Only in a perfect world!"

When the jury is ushered in I notice they look at me with different eyes. Apparently Will's cross-examination accomplished its intended purpose. Hopefully, his opening statement will be as effective.

When Will takes the podium he waits a few moments for the courtroom to quiet down. In the wake of the hush, he begins, "Ladies and gentlemen, we thank you for your service as jurors. Because the prosecution has the burden of proving Mr. Ballard's guilt, its protocol that they get to make their opening statement first. Now it's defense's turn to make an opening statement and present witnesses. Even though we are not required to do so we think it only fair that you have the full story before you're required to render a verdict. You'll find there's another side to the story.

"The first witness we will call is an individual the investigators from the Boulder County Sheriff's Office admit they did not interview. Gladys Gerard, mother of Denton's wife Penny, will testify that her daughter could sometimes be vindictive and unpredictable. She will testify that while still in high school Penny, for example, disappeared for several days when she became upset with her parents. She will testify the disappearance was similar to the disappearance the prosecution has labeled a murder. She will further testify that if her daughter perceived her husband was unfaithful she certainly was capable of staging her own disappearance as a way to make him suffer.

"The second witness we will call is Penny's father, Harry Gerard. He was present when, shortly after Penny's disappearance, a safe located in the Ballard home was found with the door ajar and the contents missing. He will testify the safe contained money Penny inherited from a great aunt and was enough to live on for several years. He will also testify that Penny was rebellious and prone to running away when things didn't suit her.

"The third witness who will be called will be Denton's receptionist, Jill Caragon. Ms. Caragon will testify that the day after Denton left for Cincinnati she received a package in the mail from Penny addressed to her boss Denton Ballard or Denny as he was sometimes called. It was postmarked the day before he left for Cincinnati. She will further testify she was present when Denton opened the package upon his return from Cincinnati and retrieved a stuffed panda bear. She will also testify he became emotional when he saw what the package contained.

"The last witness the defense will call is Penny's sister Kay Hudson. Kay will testify that the name of the bear was Kamanda, named after her and her twin sister Amanda. She will testify that she was present when Denton won the bear at a carnival and presented it to Penny along with his fraternity pin when the two of

122

them had first started going together. She will further testify that she examined Kamanda shortly after Penny's disappearance and retrieved from a secret pocket Penny's engagement and wedding rings along with Denton's fraternity pin.

"It's up to you ladies and gentlemen to draw what conclusions you will in regard to Penny having returned her engagement and wedding rings along with Denton's fraternity pin in light of her suspicions and then her disappearance."

Penny's assets were assigned to her sisters. She apparently had decided the marriage was over by leaving her engagement and wedding rings behind. In essence she was divorcing me. If I were a juror I'd conclude that since I had nothing to gain from her death, why would I kill her? And why would a juror convict with such scanty evidence?

The witnesses lived up to their billing. Debow's cross-examination was ineffective and he succeeded only in bolstering our case and in antagonizing the jury especially when he cross-examined Penny's mother.

"Mrs. Gerard, you don't really know what happened to your daughter, do you?"

"I just hope she's somewhere safe and sound and that she'll have sense enough to return so that we can all breathe more easily."

"Please just answer the question."

Mrs. Gerard leans forward placing her forearms on the railing that encloses the witness stand and glares at Debow. She answers very distinctly in a loud voice, "No, I don't; no more than you do."

"Judge, would you instruct the witness to just answer the question," Debow growls in desperation.

"I think she's done that Mr. Debow."

Debow does a poor job of hiding his embarrassment at being chastised by the judge. Glancing at his notes, apparently in an attempt to regain his composure, he then asks, "Mrs. Gerard when was the last time you heard from Penny?"

"On the Saturday before Denny was due home from Cincinnati. She said she was going hiking with some friends."

Well, that pretty much verifies Penny was alive on the Saturday before I returned on Sunday. Even I, a layman, can't believe Debow would be dumb enough to pursue that line of questioning, especially without knowing what the answer was going to be. Will taught me that 'you never ask the question unless you know the answer.'

My musings are interrupted when Debow almost shouts, "Your Honor, we ask that you strike the witness's last statement. It's hearsay. We ask that you instruct the jury to disregard it."

"*You* really opened the door by the question you asked, Mr. Debow. However since it is hearsay, the jury is instructed to disregard the last statement."

"Which one was that?" one of the jurors asks.

"Mrs. Gerard's testimony that her daughter, Penny Ballard, told her she was going hiking with her friends."

Apparently having won one, Debow is back in charge. He looks smugly back at our table as he asks, "You never told the investigating officers any of this, did you?"

"No, I was never interviewed."

That had to hurt!

"No further questions, Your Honor," Debow says and slinks back to the prosecution table.

Harry Gerard, Penny's father, is the next witness called by the defense. He pretty much follows the script outlined in Will's opening statement. He is somewhat emotional. Debow on cross succeeds only in antagonizing the jury and in garnering sympathy for Penny's father.

"Mr. Gerard," Debow begins. "Do you realize you're testifying in behalf of the man who might be responsible for your daughter's disappearance?"

"He had nothing to do with it. It's not the first time Penny has disappeared in protest to some imagined mistreatment."

"You sound like you're harboring some resentment toward your daughter."

"Not at all. I love my daughter with all my heart and I know my son-in-law does as well. I just know Penny can be vindictive and unpredictable."

"Is that based on a single incident that occurred when Penny was in high school?"

"No. There were other incidents I'm sorry to say, that caused her mother and me great concern. I'd rather not get into the details."

"Does your son-in-law have a temper?"

"Not that I'm aware of."

"On direct, you testified you and the defendant discovered that the home safe had been broken into and the contents were missing."

"I didn't say the safe had been broken into. I said the door was ajar and the contents were missing."

"How is it you know what the contents were?"

"Penny showed me the contents on several occasions and I knew she didn't trust banks and kept in her safe around one hundred thousand dollars in cash that she inherited from her great aunt on my wife's side of the family."

"Did she keep the safe locked?"

"Absolutely!"

"How is it you had access?"

"I gave her a diamond ring that had belonged to my mother, her grandmother, and was there when she placed it in the safe."

"Who had the combination?"

"As far as I know, she was the only one."

"Did the defendant also have the combination?"

"I doubt he did. Everything in the safe was Penny's."

"One too many questions," Will whispers to me.

"I guess so," I whisper back.

"No further questions," Debow says. When he walks back to his seat at the prosecution's table, his shoulders sag and he's obviously aware of his blunder.

Our third witness, Jill Caragon, testifies exactly as expected. She identifies Kamanda as the panda bear I removed from the box mailed to my office. She becomes emotional in describing my reaction when I discovered the contents of the package from Penny. She holds up well under cross-examination.

"Ms. Caragon," Debow begins, "is it unusual for a receptionist to hang around after delivering mail to management?"

"Yes. I usually just put Mr. Ballard's mail on his desk."

"Then how is it you were present when Mr. Ballard opened the package?"

"When I delivered the box, Mr. Ballard asked me to wait while he opened it."

"Hmm. Did that strike you as odd?"

"At the time it did but when he told me about his wife's disappearance I understood why."

"The reason?"

"He probably thought the box held a clue to his wife's disappearance and he wanted me there to give him moral support."

"Do you know that for a fact?"

"No. I thought you wanted my opinion."

I watch Will stifle a chuckle.

"It's possible, is it not, that Mr. Ballard sent the panda bear to himself?"

"No. The package was sealed when he opened it and the handwriting on the address label was definitely Penny's."

"When you say it was Penny's handwriting, I assume that's also your opinion?"

"I'm not a handwriting expert but I'm familiar with Penny's handwriting having watched her write on numerous occasions. She has a unique style of writing and the writing on the address label was definitely hers."

"But you didn't keep the packaging for verification did you?"

"You asked me earlier about our custom. It was our custom to throw away the packaging which we did in this case. If we knew it was going to be important we'd have kept it."

"I direct your attention to the stuffed animal you identified as being in the box mailed to Mr. Ballard's office and wrapped in the packaging you described that was never retained marked Defendant's Exhibit #1. How is it that you recognize it as the same one removed from the package you say was mailed to Mr. Ballard's office?"

"It has what looks like a red ink spot on the side of its head. If it's not the same one then it's identical to it."

"Your Honor, we object to the introduction of Defendant's Exhibit #1 into evidence. There's no proof it's one and the same panda bear as the one the witness testified to."

"It's not been offered into evidence, am I correct Mr. Crowley?" Judge Stockton says.

"No, Your Honor," Will says. "We'll be offering it through another witness."

Judge Stockton squints, "Any further questions of this witness, Mr. Debow?"

"Thank you, no further questions," Debow responds.

When Kay is called she testifies as to her having found Penny's engagement and wedding rings along with my fraternity pin in Kamanda's secret pocket. She identifies the red ink spot as one she accidently placed there. Kamanda is offered and admitted into evidence and circulated among the jurors. It's the only piece of physical evidence circulated among the jurors by the defense. A photograph of Penny had been introduced by the prosecution and circulated among the jurors in their case-in-chief. There was no other physical evidence such as a murder weapon, blood splatters, bloody or torn clothing, hair, skin or documents—which is somewhat unusual especially in a murder prosecution according to Will.

"No smoking gun," he would later say. "The prosecution fully expected you to testify and establish motive through the witnesses they held in reserve. Since that didn't happen Debow is left holding the bag."

The youngest juror, when it was time for her to examine Kamanda, looked at me and tears filled her eyes. I had to look away for I too was overcome with emotion. Kamanda was my show of love for Penny and a symbol of commitment that I had vowed never would be compromised. It was a covenant I broke when I had the affair with Twyla. If only I could turn back the clock and opt for the sacred instead of the salacious.

You'd think Kamanda was a revered relic the way Kamanda was handled by the jurors. Several of them unzipped the secret pocket and examined Penny's engagement and wedding rings and my fraternity pin. The reaction of the jury was hard to read but it was obvious they were affected by their encounter with Kamanda and their struggle to find an explanation as to why Kamanda would have been mailed to me around the time of Penny's disappearance. The inescapable explanation is and was that Penny was calling the marriage quits and what better way to convey her displeasure with me than by returning something that was dear to the both of us.

The third day of trial ended in a flurry with Debow's cross-examination of Kay.

"Mrs. Hudson, when your father testified I asked him if he realized he was testifying in behalf of the man who might be responsible for your sister's disappearance. Now I'm asking you the same question."

"Amanda and I were the little sisters Uncle Denny never had. He treated Penny and the two of us like queens. He wouldn't hurt a flea. Even when Penny was moody, which she was quite often, he never lost his cool."

"Please just answer the question!"

"If you're suggesting Uncle Denny had something to do with Penny's disappearance, then I would say you don't know Penny."

"What I'm suggesting is that your uncle *may have* had something to do with your sister's disappearance."

"Then you haven't done your homework, Mr. Debow. The unpredictable one was my sister not my uncle."

"Your Honor, the prosecution would ask that you instruct the witness to answer the question."

"Mr. Debow, the witness *is* answering the question." Judge Stockton looks rankled. "She's telling you she doesn't believe the defendant is responsible for her sister's disappearance. Please get on with it and ask another question. The court doesn't have all day."

"No further questions," Debow says as he takes his seat and folds his arms.

"He's not a happy camper," Will whispers to me.

I nod and smile.

The fourth day, the attorneys are poised to give their closing arguments. Both my parents and in-laws are present in court along with Penny's sisters and their husbands. My confidence was bolstered by the evidence or should I say the lack of evidence on the part of the prosecution.

Debow's strut hasn't changed since the first day of trial. His confidence is not contagious and the jurors do not seem to be paying attention when he speaks.

"Ladies and gentlemen," Debow begins. "Let me thank you for your service. The role played by the jury is just as important as the participants in this case. In fact when the case is turned over to you, ladies and gentlemen, the role you play will be the most important of all.

"Judge Stockton has instructed you on the law. By the way, each of you will be provided with a set of the instructions you can take back with you to the deliberation room. You should review them before you deliberate.

"One of the instructions says circumstantial evidence is just as good as direct evidence. The mere fact that no one saw Mr. Ballard kill his wife doesn't mean he didn't. The circumstantial evidence says otherwise.

"To begin with it's odd defendant didn't take his wife with him to Cincinnati and instead was accompanied by his secretary. It's odd no one saw his wife after he left for Cincinnati. It's even more of an oddity that defendant's wife just disappeared into thin air without leaving a trace and leaving behind all her personal belongings including her wallet and SUV.

"When defendant was interviewed by sheriff's deputies he told them his wife had accused him of having an affair with his secretary and was upset when he left for Cincinnati with his secretary. With no evidence of a break-in, the investigators concluded no third parties were involved in the disappearance of defendant's wife.

"The defense will no doubt argue that with no body having been discovered, there's no evidence of death. The prosecution would submit that in every case where a defendant successfully disposes of a body so that it can't be found, there'd never be a conviction and the defendant would be free to kill again. We're asking that you not allow that to happen.

"By causing his wife's death, defendant is guilty of first degree murder. By concealing her body, defendant is guilty of concealing a death. By lying to the sheriff's deputies and leading them to believe his wife was missing and still alive he's guilty of false reporting and obstructing justice. We're asking you to return guilty verdicts not because the prosecution is asking you to do so but because justice cries out for it."

As soon as Debow sits down Judge Stockton looks at Will. "Mr. Crowley..."

Will nods and stands. Buttoning his suit jacket he takes the podium. "Ladies and gentlemen I too want to thank you for your service. A jury consisting of one's peers is the method the founders of our Constitution devised to make sure innocent citizens of our great country are not unjustly convicted and whether a person is guilty or not guilty is not left to the whims and caprice of a prosecuting attorney like Mr. Debow. It's a screening device if you will and our system of justice has been and remains the best system in the world."

Will pauses momentarily. He leans a forearm on the podium and continues, "How do you prove a negative? Sometimes all you can do is say you didn't do what you've been accused of doing. Mr. Ballard did that when he was interviewed by Deputies Fuller and Whittaker. He told them he had nothing to do with his wife's disappearance—that he loved her and would do nothing to harm her. He also did that by his plea of *not guilty* to all the charges in this case." Will turns and looks at me. "As he sits here in court today Denton Ballard rests on the presumption of innocence afforded him by the Constitution. How *do* you prove a negative? Only by what he's already said—he didn't do what he's been accused of! By law, it's the responsibility of the prosecution to prove beyond a reasonable doubt that he did—not the other way around.

"Has the prosecution met their burden? Mr.Debow says they have. But his opinion like mine doesn't count. It's the evidence, or the lack of evidence, that's been produced or not produced here at trial that determines whether Denton Ballard is guilty or not guilty. What evidence is there that Penny Ballard is even deceased? Are you convinced beyond a reasonable doubt that she is?

"Even though, unlike the prosecution, the defense does not have to prove anything we called witnesses in order to show that Penny was vindictive and staged her disappearance out of spite. When Penny perceived her husband was cheating on her, she did what her mother said she did when she was in high school and was upset with someone or something. She disappeared without a trace. It was her way to punish her parents then and her way now to punish her husband. She returned home back then. Will she re-

turn home someday when she thinks her husband has been suffi-
ciently punished for his alleged affair? Are you convinced beyond
a reasonable doubt she won't? Is it just a coincidence that she disappeared at least twice that we know of to punish those who love
her when she didn't get her way?

"If Denton Ballard killed his wife why wouldn't he have disposed of her personal belongings to make it appear she ran off?
Or why didn't he stage the scene to make it appear she was abducted? The only thing that was missing from the family home
was the large amount of cash in the safe to which only Penny had
the combination—a tidy sum she could live on for quite some
time. Was the so-called insurance policy Penny's key to a new life
and a way to punish her husband?

"I ask you to call your common sense into play. Isn't it more
likely Penny staged the scene to make it appear she was the victim
of foul play to make her husband sweat and then to reappear after he'd done his penance? Has the prosecution proven to you beyond any reasonable doubt that that didn't happen or that Penny
was not abducted and that Denton Ballard killed his wife?

"You might say that the alternative scenario is farfetched.
The uncontradicted testimony in the record is that Penny ar-
ranged for a package containing a stuffed panda bear named Kamanda to be sent to her husband's business and to arrive while
he was in Cincinnati. Kamanda was not just any stuffed animal. It
had a secret pocket containing her engagement and wedding rings
and a fraternity pin presented to her by her future husband shortly after they met. What was the symbolism in returning the panda Denton Ballard won for her and the other cherished items? To
express her displeasure when her husband's secretary accompanied him on the business trip to Cincinnati. Obviously—another
way to punish him.

"If you're convinced beyond any and all reasonable doubt that Denton Ballard murdered his wife and covered up her death and lied to sheriff's deputies when he said he didn't know what happened to her and denied being involved in her disappearance then you should find him guilty on all counts. On the other hand, if you feel the prosecution did not meet its burden of proof and didn't prove Denton Ballard's guilt beyond a reasonable doubt then you are bound by law to return a not guilty verdict on all counts. And that's what we're asking you to do."

Jury deliberations consumed the better part of the fifth day of trial. It was around 4:00 p.m. when I was notified the jury had reached a verdict. I was immediately transported from the El Paso County Jail where I was being held to the El Paso County Justice Center. Will had notified my parents, Penny's parents and sisters that the jury had reached a verdict. They, together with Kay's and Amanda's husbands were present in court when I arrived. So were Will and Jessica. Not surprisingly, one of the reporters from the *Erie Chronicle* was also present.

Will was reserved and a drastic contrast from Debow who was already celebrating what he no doubt thought was another victory. "He'll be wiping the smile off his face," Will says, "as soon as the verdict is read. His confidence will be shattered before he leaves the courtroom."

"You really think so?" I ask Will uncertain his prediction is correct but hoping it is.

"I guarantee it!" he says and looks at me sternly. "Your case should never have gone this far."

When the foreman hands the verdict form to the bailiff and the bailiff hands it to Judge Stockton and Judge Stockton reads it before announcing the verdict, I quit breathing. I search her face for a reaction. She is somber and in a steady voice she reads the verdict. "We the jury duly impaneled and sworn do find the defendant Denton Ballard...*not guilty* on all counts."

My blood is pounding so loudly in my ears I'm not sure I heard the verdict correctly. "Did she say *not guilty?*" I ask Will.

"You heard her right!" Will replies and places his hand on my shoulder. "Half of your worries are over!"

I'm suddenly elated but only for a few seconds as I remember I'm facing another murder trial on the horizon. "What about my pending murder case involving Twyla?"

"Evidence ain't any better in that case. We'll ask that you be released on bond in light of the verdict in this case. However, don't count on our request being granted."

When my support group starts to mob me, Judge Stockton bangs her gavel and calls the court to order. "If there are any further outbursts, I'll clear the courtroom," she says in a harsh voice.

"Do you wish the jury polled, Mr. Debow?"

"Yes, Your Honor."

Each juror is then asked, "Was and is this your verdict?" All answer "yes." The jury is then excused with the thanks of the court.

After the jury has been excused, Judge Stockton says to Will, "I assume you'll be asking the court to release Mr. Ballard on bond in the murder prosecution of Twyla Marin?"

"Yes, Your Honor. We make that motion!" Will says and his eyes light up.

"Any objection, Mr. Debow?"

"Yes, Your Honor. The key witness in this case is the victim in that case. But for the unavailability of Twyla Marin in this case the verdict in all likelihood would have been much different."

Judge Stockton looks at Will and says, "What say you, Mr. Crowley?"

"Your Honor, the evidence in the Marin case is not any stronger than the evidence in the case just concluded. In fact it's weaker. The proof is not evident and the presumption is not great in that case. Mr. Ballard has already been incarcerated for almost six months on a bogus murder charge. Justice would not be best served by locking him up for another six months on still another bogus murder charge. He's not a flight risk, has no criminal convictions and it is unlikely he'll be convicted in the Marin case."

"Mr. Crowley, the court would be remiss if it made the same mistake twice. It was while your client was out on bond—not a popular move on my part—that the key witness in the case just concluded mysteriously disappeared. We can't risk another witness *disappearing* now can we?"

Not a popular move on her part! Sounds like she's pandering to public opinion rather than making a rational independent decision.

When I turn to Will he's already on his feet addressing the court. "Your Honor, you're assuming Mr. Ballard somehow was involved in Ms. Marin's disappearance. Last I heard an accused is presumed innocent and entitled to be placed on bond pending a conviction except in a first degree murder case where the proof is evidence and the presumption great. As in the case just concluded, there is no evidence either direct or indirect that Ms. Marin is deceased let alone evidence that Mr. Ballard was somehow involved. Unless the legislature in its infinite wisdom changed the law, speculation and conjecture are in the *guess* category and being considered mere suspicion or supposition do not a conviction make."

By the expression on the judge's face and her tone of voice I get the impression Will is not making points. Probably not a good idea to lecture a judge on the law.

"Mr. Crowley, weighing your client's interest against the public's welfare, I cannot in good conscience grant your request. It's not my job to determine innocence or guilt. That would be invading the province of the jury. It's therefore my order that Mr. Ballard remain in the custody of the sheriff of Boulder County until such time as there has been a resolution in the new prosecution."

My euphoria is short-lived. To spend more time in a human-sized bird cage for a crime I didn't commit is almost too much to bear. *Guess my indiscretion with Twyla came with a price!*

When I'm returned to the Boulder County Jail the following day, Will is waiting for me. He is allowed to accompany me to my cell. He hands me a copy of the morning newspaper. The headline reads:

BALLARD FOUND NOT GUILTY IN MURDER OF WIFE

The story that follows reads:

> After a week-long trial and eight hours of deliberation, an El Paso County jury found Erie businessman Denton Ballard not guilty of all charges in connection with the disappearance and presumed death of his wife, Penny. Ballard was charged with first degree murder and three other related charges. The first degree murder charge carried with it a possible penalty of life imprisonment or death.
>
> Ballard's parents and in-laws were present when the verdicts were read. The victim's parents, Mr. and Mrs. Harry Gerard and one of Penny's younger sisters, Kay Hudson, had testified in Ballard's behalf during the trial. They painted the victim as vindictive with a propensity to disappear

when things didn't go her way. When interviewed by a reporter from the *Erie Chronicle*, the victim's father stated 'In my heart I know Penny is out there somewhere and will be returning someday when she gets good and ready.' Mr. Gerard declined to answer any further questions.

When District Attorney Arthur Debow was interviewed, he stated, 'Without a body or any physical evidence to tie Mr. Ballard into his wife's disappearance, we knew we had an uphill battle. And without the testimony of our star witness, who also mysteriously disappeared, we knew the chances of obtaining a conviction were little to none. Since I took an oath to uphold the law, I had no choice but to proceed with or without our star witness.'

A pensive Willard Crowley, Ballard's attorney said he was disappointed with a system that allowed an innocent man to be subjected to incarceration prior to trial and prosecution without any evidence. 'If the trauma of his wife's disappearance wasn't enough, he [Denton Ballard] had to suffer a persecution he didn't deserve in the media and in court.' Ballard still faces criminal prosecution in the disappearance of his longtime secretary, Twyla Marin. His request to be released on bond pending trial in the second case was denied.

10

PEOPLE v. BALLARD II

AS A CHILD I'd lay on my back in the grass and spend idle hours watching clouds drift across the sky. The various shapes resembled polar bears, bearded faces and poodles. Time seemed to stand still and I didn't have a care in the world.

When I got older, time was on a fast track and I tried to squeeze as much into a twenty-four hour day as I could. There was a time when I felt I was caught up in the tide and had no control over my life. I let nature take its course and the hell with the consequences. I spent less time thinking and more time doing. Now, I spend more time thinking and less time doing.

Being in lockup has its advantages and its disadvantages. However, once you catch up on your reading you only have time on your hands—time to think and time to obsess. How could Penny be so insensitive as to let me rot in prison to settle a score? On the other hand how could I have been so insensitive as to be unfaithful to the woman who had placed her implicit faith in me and believed my denials and excuses?

Guess the only person I fooled was myself. How can I blame Penny for the predicament in which I find myself? I deserve to suffer in hell and being locked in a cage not much bigger than a dog pen without privacy or peace of mind is certainly hell or the closest thing to it.

I never really loved Twyla like I loved Penny. It was a prurient interest I had in Twyla—an unhealthy fascination that spiraled wildly out of control. It was not mind over matter but an irresistible impulse that consumed me and led me down a path of destruction. I know better now but I didn't then when indiscretion and deceit were my masters and the temptation was too great to resist.

Looking back, the only one I snookered was myself. Selling myself out for thirty pieces of silver like Judas comes with it the same price—eternal damnation and suffering commensurate with the sellout. Roy may get his wish after all.

I'm sitting on the edge of my cot and don't even look up when Will comes in. "Why so glum chum?" he asks. "We won the tough one. Debow is pretty demoralized by your acquittal in Penny's case."

"I don't feel victorious. Maybe I deserve the death penalty," I say. "I've ruined a lot of lives."

"Are you crazy? Maybe the insanity defense isn't so absurd after all."

"Will, I've had a lot of time to think," I say as I walk to the bars and look out into the jail version of the boardwalk. Will follows my movement with concern written on his face.

"What's up, partner?" he asks.

I turn to face him. "On the one hand I'm upset with Penny and on the other hand I'm upset with myself. I'm sure Penny has been following the case and gloating over her slight-of-hand trick. Can't help wondering what would have happened if I'd been convicted and sentenced to die. Would she have emerged from the woodwork in time to save my sorry ass or would she have relished in my execution? It's one thing to watch me squirm and another thing to watch me die."

Will fires back at me, "And do you think you deserve to die for being unfaithful?"

"Debow did. So did the press."

"That was when you were suspected of killing Penny to enhance your relationship with Twyla—not for having the affair."

"And it appears Penny and Twyla's husband did as well. Anyway, same difference. In a way I *killed* them both with my philandering ways. Neither one of their lives will be the same."

Shaking his head, Will persists, "That's not what your relatives and friends think and they're the ones who really matter."

I sit back down on my cot. Will's reassurance does little to change my mood. "Has Stockton set Twyla's trial date yet?"

Will sits down beside me. "I've filed a motion to exclude Twyla's hearsay statements and several other motions in your behalf. Debow opposes the hearsay motion but admits it would be error for the court not to grant it. He doesn't want to build error in the case and risk reversal on appeal should he get a conviction."

I cringe at the thought. "What are the chances of a conviction?"

"Without Twyla's hearsay statements to the S.O. and without her apparent confession to her husband, the prosecution doesn't have much of a case—assuming you don't testify."

"You think I can win this one, too, without testifying?"

"Yep. You did in Penny's case and that case was much stronger than Twyla's. Their theory is that murdering Twyla was your way to silence her. Since only you and Twyla knew the two of you were having an affair, only you and Twyla can testify to that fact."

"Since I'm not going to testify and Twyla is not available to testify, the affair can't come in, right?"

"The only evidence they have is that Twyla was a key prosecution witness in your criminal case and you presumably were the last person to be with her before she disappeared. They will try to get the no contact order into evidence but we will oppose it on the grounds that the probative value is outweighed by the prejudicial effect and in essence would require you to waive your Fifth Amendment right in asserting that Twyla was the one who first made contact. Should that fail, we can still call Jill Caragon who will testify to Twyla's telephone call and her coming to your office. The tradeoff is that Jill will testify that the two of you left together. Jill's *good* testimony far outweighs the *bad*. Besides, Renee Stapleton saw the two of you together at the coffee shop after Twyla came to your office."

"Are you saying reference to the no contact order will probably be allowed into evidence even though it was Twyla who initiated the contact?"

"The Fifth Amendment argument probably won't fly since there is an alternate way for us to show who made the first contact without you having to testify. We'll make the argument to ensure a record is made in case of an appeal."

"How about me passing the polygraph? Shouldn't that count for something? Are you still going to try to get that before the jury?"

"It's a futile effort and like our attempt in Penny's case, it will be summarily denied."

At the motions hearing Will succeeds in keeping out Twyla's hearsay statements including those to her husband and to the police. That means if I don't testify the jury will not be informed of our affair. Of no lesser significance is that the prosecution will be precluded from referring to Penny's case or that I was a suspect in Penny's disappearance. Without argument, Will's motion for change of venue is granted. Twyla's case, as was Penny's, is transferred to Colorado Springs. *A good omen!*

Will's motion to prevent the prosecution from referring to Twyla as a *key* or *star* witness in a case against me is denied. "It shows motive," Judge Stockton says, "and an indispensable part of the prosecution's case." With regard to Twyla's civil case, Judge Stockton rules, "Any reference to that case by the prosecution or that it was even filed will be grounds for a mistrial."

When the judge mentions mistrial, I glance over at Debow who is seated at the prosecution table. He doesn't show any emotion but keeps his head down as he jots notes on a legal pad.

Turning to Will, Judge Stockton asks, "Mr. Crowley, will you stipulate that Twyla Marin, the alleged victim in this case, was an endorsed witness in another court case against your client or do you want the prosecution to call the court clerk to establish that fact?"

"We so stipulate," Will replies. Then to me he whispers, "Don't want court personnel testifying in behalf of the prosecution. That will just lend more credence to their case." Will pauses then adds, "It will be interesting to see how the prosecution will prove Twyla was an indispensable witness without calling a member of the DA's staff as a witness to testify to that fact. They can't be a prosecutor and a witness at the same time—conflict of interest." Will shoots me an evil grin. His look convinces me Debow has painted himself into still another corner.

The judge continues ruling on the motions. The no contact order is deemed admissible and my polygraph results inadmissible. "Win some; lose some," Will says. Judge Stockton sets my trial for two weeks commencing at 8:00 a.m. on Monday, March 19, 2018.

"Apprehensive?" Will asks.

"Sort of, but this isn't my first rodeo!" I reply.

We both laugh.

Since the prosecution is not asking for the death penalty—a change in tactics on their part—jury selection is relatively unremarkable. Seven men and five women, all under the age of fifty are selected. Only one has prior jury service and the rest are unfamiliar with the judicial system.

After making a brief opening statement, Debow calls Fuller and Whittaker to the stand. In what appears to be rehearsed testimony, Fuller, over Will's objection, gets in the fact that Twyla was a critical witness in the court case against me at the time of her disappearance.

"Looks like Stockton is going out of her way to gerrymander a conviction," Will whispers to me.

Fuller and Whittaker set the stage and testify as to Twyla's disappearance and the no contact order issued by the court. Jill Caragon, the third witness called by the prosecution, testifies that Twyla was a former secretary at Azar Publishers. She also recounts that on the day Twyla disappeared Twyla came into my office unannounced and the two of us left for coffee at approximately 11:00 a.m. She testifies that I returned to the office about 1:00 p.m.

The next prosecution witness is Renee Stapleton. She testifies Twyla and I came into the Sunlight Coffee Station where she works as a waitress a little after 11:00 a.m. and ordered a Danish and a cup of coffee. When asked how she remembered the time she stated that it was right before her eleven o'clock lunch break but because the other waitresses were swamped she took our order. She testifies that she was familiar with the employees of Azar Publishers as we were *regulars* at Sunlight. After she identifies me as Twyla's escort, Debow hands her a photograph of Twyla.

"Is this a photograph of the person you knew as Twyla and the person who was in the company of Mr. Ballard?"

"Yes. They came into the Sunlight together a lot."

"Are you sure?" Debow asks.

Déjà vu. The same feelings of despair swarm me.

"Absolutely!" Renee responds. "In fact she's the lady coming into the courtroom right now," Renee says and points to the door leading into the courtroom.

I'm not the only one who gasps when we all turn our attention to the rear of the courtroom. All hell breaks loose, and between the spectators and the media, chaos reigns supreme. Judge Stockton bangs her gavel and her shouts for order are universally ignored.

I'm feeling somewhat vindicated that my murder victim suddenly appears alive and well. In the midst of the bedlam I glance over at Debow. His expression is priceless. He looks like he just saw a ghost.

Judge Stockton beckons for Twyla to come forward. As Twyla does so, Judge Stockton asks Debow, "Is this the person you claim Mr. Ballard murdered?" Judge Stockton doesn't look too pleased to say the least. In fact I would describe her as livid.

"I'm afraid so," Debow responds.

"You better be afraid," Judge Stockton scolds.

When Debow doesn't respond, Judge Stockton says, "Your rush to judgment in bringing murder charges against Mr. Ballard was a bit premature wouldn't you say?"

Debow remains silent. Now he's looking for that hole to crawl into.

Addressing Twyla who is now standing a few feet from the bench, Judge Stockton says, "Can you tell us who you are?"

Without hesitation, Twyla says, "I'm Twyla Marin."

The judge adjusts her glasses and leans forward on the bench, "Why haven't you made your presence known before now?"

I notice Twyla has avoided any eye contact with me. Now she shifts from foot to foot and finally says, "I just got back to Colorado and when I learned of the trial I immediately drove here from Erie."

"You have caused quite a stir by your absence, do you realize that?"

"I didn't until my husband told me."

"And how is it that not even your husband knew of your whereabouts? Surely he must have been frantic about what happened to you."

"Roy and I had a knock down-drag out argument and I left him. I didn't tell him where I was going because I didn't want him to follow me. I needed space and time to think things over. Since I was out of the country, I didn't have access to any news happening in the U.S."

Judge Stockton nods and then directs her remarks at Debow.

"Looks like you and your investigators have egg on your faces. At first blush it appeared the investigation was thorough and you had the evidence to support the charges. Unfortunately, you bypassed the preliminary hearing and opted to take the case before the grand jury. If you had had a preliminary hearing instead, we would have discovered how weak the case was and headed it off before it went this far. We could have saved Mr. Ballard and everyone else a lot of heartache." Judge Stockton glares at Debow and adds, "Don't be surprised if Mr. Ballard brings a civil action against you and your office alleging false arrest, malicious prosecution and false imprisonment. Just hope I'm not the judge assigned that case."

Looking at Will, Judge Stockton says, "I assume in light of the circumstances you will be asking me to dismiss all the charges against Mr. Ballard *with prejudice*." The judge looks at the jury and explains, "*With prejudice* means the charges can never be filed again." Then looking back at Will she continues, "I anticipate a request for an order releasing Mr. Ballard from custody as well."

"We now make such a motion, Your Honor."

"Any objection, Mr. Debow?"

"No, Your Honor." Debow keeps his head lowered when he answers the judge. If he weren't such an ass I would feel sorry for him.

The judge straightens herself and scowls at the press corps. "I'm going to enter my order concerning this case. I'm giving you fair warning that if you disrupt this courtroom proceedings before I adjourn, there will be severe consequences for you and your employers."

The venue is so quiet you could hear a pin drop. The judge adjusts her robe around her ample bosom and continues, "Very well then, the court enters an order that all charges against Mr. Ballard are hereby dismissed with prejudice and the request for release from custody is hereby granted." When Stockton smiles at me from her perch, apparently looking for some sign of gratitude, I suddenly remember how she tried to railroad me and now it's my turn to ignore her. I look away and remain stoic hoping she interprets my slight as an insult.

To the jury, Judge Stockton says, "The court did not dismiss you earlier in order to afford you the opportunity to see firsthand how our system of justice works and that justice is swift. At this time you are released from any further jury duty in this case with my thanks. Your service is much appreciated. The bailiff will now escort you back to the jury room so you can collect your personal belongings."

As soon as the jury leaves, Judge Stockton says, "Mr. Ballard, your taste of the criminal justice system understandably has been a bitter one. You've had to endure not one but two jury trials that ended in your favor. Hopefully it, together with the time you served, will prove to you there are no shortcuts in life and that discretion as they say is the better part of valor."

I bite my tongue to keep from addressing the judge's lecture on how I should be grateful for the reprieve. I'm still a little miffed by being falsely accused. But for my illicit affair with Twyla none of this would have happened. So the only one I have to blame is myself but I wonder how many people in this courtroom have had or are involved in extramarital affairs.

I look at Twyla who has taken a seat in the front row. Because of the no contact order I can't speak to her and even Will agrees that Twyla probably knows where Penny is.

Judge Stockton bangs her gavel and announces "Court is now adjourned."

Suddenly the courtroom erupts in mayhem as the reporters run across each other scrambling out the doors.

Will chuckles. "You'll no doubt make the front page again," he says and claps me on the back.

I breathe a sigh of relief.

The headlines in the morning edition of the *Erie Chronicle* read:

VICTIM IN MURDER PROSECUTION APPEARS IN COURT

The lead story reads:

As unlikely as it seems, the alleged victim was seated in the courtroom in the criminal prosecution of businessman Denton Ballard and identified by a witness as the person she knew as Twyla Marin. 'It was like a scene from a movie,' a cameraman from one of the local television stations was heard to say. 'The victim of the criminal homicide appeared in court to watch the trial of the man accused of her murder. How often does that happen?'

The surprise appearance in the courtroom by Twyla Marin caused quite a stir when Renee Stapleton, a waitress at the Sunlight Coffee Station, pointed her out and identified Marin as the person seen with Denton Ballard on the date of Marin's disappearance. When Marin was identified by Stapleton, chaos erupted in the courtroom and Judge Madeline Stockton banged her gavel several long minutes in an effort to restore order.

Ballard was charged with murder in the death of his wife Penny in a case that was transferred to Colorado Springs in November of last year. At the end of a week-long trial Ballard was found not guilty of all charges. Penny's body was never found. When Twyla Marin, a key witness in that case also disappeared, Ballard was charged with her murder. Ballard had entered not guilty pleas in both cases.

Upon the appearance of Marin, the case against Ballard for her murder was summarily dismissed and Ballard was ordered released from custody where he had remained for the past nine months. In addressing District Attorney Arthur Debow, Judge Stockton said, 'Your rush to judgment in bringing murder charges was a bit premature wouldn't you say?'

When asked why she hadn't made her presence known before, Marin stated, 'I just got back to Colorado and when I learned of the trial I immediately drove here from Erie.' Her reason for having disappeared? "Roy [Marin's husband] and I had a knock down-drag out argument and I left him. I didn't tell him where I was going because I didn't want him to follow me. I needed space and time to think things over. Since I was out of the country, I didn't have access to any news happening in the U.S."

Ballard's attorney, Will Crowley, when asked by the *Erie Chronicle* if his client was considering a civil action against the district attorney's office and the investigating officers for false arrest, false imprisonment and malicious prosecution said: 'That's certainly a possibility and warranted under the circumstances. However, our focus right now is locating Penny."

Debow told the *Erie Chronicle* that he felt compelled to prosecute Ballard since the charges were brought by grand jury indictment and his office was pressured by Marin's husband to do so.

The editorial also demonstrated a change of heart.

KAMANDA

RUSH TO JUDGMENT

The death penalty case involving local businessman Denton Ballard could have ended badly if the alleged victim Twyla Marin hadn't arrived on the scene. The disappearance of a person does not always a murder make. We ask our district attorney, Arthur Debow, the same question the presiding judge asked, 'Your rush to judgment in bringing murder charges was a bit premature wouldn't you say?"

11

PEOPLE v. BALLARD III

MY QUEST FOR vindication doesn't stop with the not guilty verdict in Penny's case nor the dismissal in Twyla's disappearance case. I feel compelled to find Penny for two reasons. One is to prove to the world that I'm innocent and the second is to determine if Penny would have let me fry if I had received the death penalty in her case. Down deep I also want very much for her to be alive and well. Was I thinking of reconciliation? Not really.

After the dust settles and things get back to near normal, I receive an anonymous call from New York State. The caller asks how Kamanda is doing. Before I can respond the caller hangs up. Niagara Falls is where Penny and I went on our honeymoon. Penny and I had talked about living on the Canadian side someday. We even met with a realtor in St. Catharines. A lightbulb goes off in my head. Canada is where Penny's best friend Megan Frey lives!

I immediately dial Will's direct line.

"Denny, what a nice surprise. I've been thinking about you. What's up?"

I tell him about the anonymous call.

"Come have lunch with me. My treat."

"How about Lydia's at eleven forty-five?"

"See you there."

It's been almost a month since the dismissal in Twyla's case. However, you'd have thought years had come and gone by the way Will and I hug and pat each other on the back when we meet.

As soon as the waitress takes our order and retreats, Will gets down to business. "Recognize the caller's voice?"

I think about it as I push the lemon wedge around in my water glass with my fork. "If you're asking if it was Penny, I couldn't say. Whoever the caller was disguised her voice."

"You say she asked how Kamanda was doing?"

"Yes."

"Think it was Penny?"

"Think it was something she would do considering the torment she's already put me through—why stop now?"

"Good point. Have you talked to her friend Megan?"

"Not since the day I returned from Cincinnati."

"Could the caller have been Megan?"

"Could've been. As you know, New York is just across the border from Canada and the two have been friends since childhood."

"Would Penny stoop to taunting you?"

"Before all of this happened I wouldn't have thought so. Now I'm not sure. If she knew I was acquitted, she might. Especially if she was out for blood."

"Uh-huh. Who else would be playing games with you?"

"In my business I don't make enemies of that caliber. The only prospects I can think of are Penny and possibly Twyla."

"Stands to reason that the caller would have in all likelihood used a payphone so that the call couldn't be traced."

"Oh, yeah! It was definitely a payphone. I heard the sound of coins being inserted into the slot."

"What say we hire a private investigator and get on this right away? If Megan is as good a friend of Penny's as you say, she could very well have lied when she said she didn't know where Penny was. She's probably hiding her."

"I thought of that and wouldn't be surprised. And also wouldn't be surprised if that's where Twyla's been hiding all this time. I'm sure Penny and Twyla did more than discuss horses and weather on the long rides they took together. Penny probably told Twyla about spending a couple of weeks every year with Megan in Canada."

"Sounds logical. Wonder how hard it would be for Twyla to talk. My lawyer instincts tell me she obviously knows more than she's saying."

"I trust your lawyer instincts, my friend. Let's do it. Maybe she'll talk to a PI."

"It's worth a try. I know just the guy for the job."

"Twyla's now working for a realtor in Erie," Will says. "I just ran across an add she has in the *Erie Chronicle* for the sale of an apartment building."

"I remember her saying she had a realtor's license. She complained that the market had bottomed out and people just liked having her run them around showing houses they couldn't afford. It was then she came to work for me."

"Right. The times were tough for realtors."

"Who did you say we could hire as an investigator?"

"Guy by the name of Tad Faraday. He's an ex-cop from the Boulder P.D. I've used him on a number of occasions over the years. He's expensive but worth every penny—if you'll excuse the pun."

"I take it he'll pose as an investor who's interested in Twyla's listing?"

"Right you are! He's very good at disguising what he really is. He's known as The Chameleon among his comrades."

"The Chameleon? Sounds mysterious and intriguing. Seems like a good place to start. Sign him up and let me know if he requires some kind of a retainer."

"I'll take care of it. In the meantime let Tad do his job and don't contact Twyla."

"I wouldn't go near her with a ten-foot pole but just for the record, am I still under the no contact order?"

"Yes. Since the judge didn't lift it, you are."

It's less than a week when I receive a call from Will. His enthusiasm is contagious when he says, "Bingo! We've hit pay dirt. Come by my office at three and I'll fill you in."

Dammit! After all these months of uncertainty, it's not fair that I have to wait until three for the gory details. I quell my disappointment and agree to the time and place. Needless to say I'm at Will's office ten minutes early. I'm immediately ushered into one of the firm's conference rooms where I'm soon joined by Will. He's all smiles.

"Doesn't hurt to hire an investigator who's tall, dark and handsome," Will says. "Tad got a tour of the building and ended up with Twyla in one of the furnished apartments. I'll skip the details but at the end of the day Twyla told all.

That slut!

Either Will didn't notice or chose to ignore the look on my face as he continues. "Penny apparently is and has been living in a condo in St. Catharine's not far from the U.S. border. She had news that Penny is living with some dude who's a musician and a song writer from Nashville."

I'm relieved at the news and say "Thank God she's alive! Did Tad get an address?"

"He's working on it. Tad says that after a few more showings at the apartment building Twyla has listed he'll have Penny's address.

"I suppose he wants hazard pay?"

Will chuckles. "He told me this one was on the house since there were so many perks."

I grin. *Being familiar with Twyla's talents, I'm thinking Tad should pay me for the referral.*

A few days later Will calls with an address. "Didn't know it'd be that easy," he says and chuckles again. "Maybe I should inquire into those apartments—strictly for an investment of course."

When I call Penny's parents with the news they are elated especially when I give them her address. Several weeks pass before I hear from them again.

"We talked Penny into coming home," Penny's mother says. "Apparently she dumped her boyfriend when she found out he was married and had several children by two different wives. So much for Prince Charming."

"When you say home, are you saying she's moving back to Erie?"

"She's going to stay with us until she figures out what to do with her life," her father who is also on the line says. "She says she's not ready for any kind of reconciliation with you or anyone else."

"I just thank God she's all right," I say. "Tell her I'm ready to talk anytime she is."

When I call Will with the latest, he acts surprised. "As I said before, I didn't think it'd be that easy," he says. "Wonder if Penny has something more up her sleeve. Remember what happened to Adam when he listened to Eve?"

"But she didn't force him to eat the apple."

"Right. But God didn't put the words 'lead us not into temptation' in the Lord's prayer for naught. He knew the nature of man."

"You're just full of surprises," I say. "When did you get so philosophical?"

"Just stick around. I'm a multi-faceted diamond and you've just scratched the surface."

"You're too much. Now getting back to our current plight," I say, "you'll be the first to know. Fool me once, shame on you. Fool me twice, shame on me."

"Let's make Penny's existence our little secret at least for the time being. We don't want a lot of gossip, speculation and adverse publicity to torpedo reconciliation if it comes to that. Both of you need time to think without interference."

"Roger that," I say.

It takes a lot of patience for me not to contact Penny. On the one hand I'd like to ask her why she left me hanging. On the other, I'd like to offer an apology for my indiscretions and beg for forgiveness. I'm so conflicted, I can't think straight.

I obsess over the fact that Penny's been shacked up with another man. For years I was bothered by the prospect that if I predeceased her she would strike up a relationship with another man. I wanted to be the only man in Penny's life. I was so possessive that if she even smiled at another man I became enraged and would make a scene. I was very accusatory and imagined all kinds of things that only drove a wedge into our relationship and may have been the reason for my infidelity.

When Penny admitted to not being a virgin when we first started going together, I thought seriously of ending the relationship. Not that I was a virgin, but I wanted my wife to be. My jealousy spoiled a lot of what should have been happy times and ruined many of our evenings out together. In fact it got so bad I'd follow her when she went shopping or to lunch with the girls. I surreptitiously checked the clothes hamper to see if there were signs of extramarital activity. I even eavesdropped on some of her telephone conversations.

To this day, I don't know what drove me. I cringe remembering one of our office Christmas parties and Penny dancing with another man. The two seemed to be having too much fun together so I went home in a jealous rage. I'm ashamed to say, I left her in the lurch to fend for herself. Maybe it's the same thing Penny did to me.

It's ironic that I suspected Penny all those years of being unfaithful when in fact I was the philanderer. The double standard wasn't fair to Penny. I know turnabout is fair play but when I think of Penny having done what I did, I'm incensed. What we did to each other was not right but her returning the favor by her infidelity of late and staging her disappearance to voice her disapproval was overkill—figuratively and almost literally. How can I be forgiven if I'm not willing to forgive? Yet…

It's been almost two months since Penny returned from St. Catharines and went to live with her parents. Although I've heard from her parents sporadically during that time, I've not heard from Penny.

Today is Friday the week before Christmas. I'm dead tired from a rough week of meeting deadlines. The publishing business is not easy and I'm dismayed I didn't finish a new novel of my own in time for the Christmas buying frenzy. Ironically it's called *The Unattainable*.

I've been a basket case since the Penny/Twyla debacle and I'm starting to question my sanity. Certainly my competency in all quarters has fallen off. There was a time I felt I may be wrong but never in doubt about my decision-making. Now I'm second-guessing everything I do. It's while in this frame of mind that I head home from the office.

Snow has been accumulating for several days and the ground is covered. The ranch is a winter wonderland and emits a certain peace I'm unable to find elsewhere. Today, whether due to loneliness or the nature of the season, the solitude is not all that alluring.

As I approach the house I see a late model SUV parked in the driveway. I don't recognize it and when I get closer I notice footprints in the snow leading to the stable where Stormy and several other horses are kept. *Hmm! That's strange.* I park behind the SUV and follow the tracks to the stable. It takes me a moment to become accustomed to the gloom after the brightness of the snow. When my vision adjusts I see a feminine figure grooming Stormy. *Can't be!* "Penny!" I shout. Her back is toward me and she turns and faces me. A big smile graces her face and it takes my breath away. I've missed her so much...

"Hey, cowboy," she says, "need a hired hand?"

I'm on the verge of tears, however I manage to reply, "Could use all the help I can get."

"So can I," Penny says but before I can read too much into that statement she adds, "I need some help with Stormy. He's stubborn and hard to handle. Go change your clothes and you can help calm him. He doesn't seem to remember me."

Excitement races through me. The months of uncertainty, torment and anxiety melt away. My only thought at this moment is that Penny has returned home!

When Penny sees my meager supply of food she suggests we go shopping and stock up. It's not unusual to get snowbound for days in Colorado's rural areas. I remember one winter the snow was so deep we became stranded and had to be rescued.

As we head for town, Penny also suggests we stop by the mall "for some last minute Christmas gifts." This talk of stocking up and Christmas gifts reminds me of the *old days* before Penny left and I'm growing nostalgic. I glance over at Penny and at that moment I wish with all my heart I could take back all the hurt and disappointment I've caused her and so many others. What in the hell was I thinking when I started the affair with Twyla? Penny and I had a pretty good life, both in and out of bed and Twyla brought nothing to my life that I didn't already have—legitimacy.

When we reach the mall, we split up and I head for the nearest jewelry store. *What do you buy a woman who has everything?* After mulling over a wide selection of expensive jewelry items I settle on a set of emerald earrings since emerald is Penny's birthstone. I have them gift wrapped and secrete the small gift box in my parka pocket. When I meet Penny at the prearranged kiosk in the center of the mall she is laden with a variety of different sized packages and gift boxes.

She looks disappointed and says, "My! You certainly were conservative. Did you just hang out at the arcade while I did the shopping?"

"My shopping habits are none of your business. Maybe I'm having my extravaganza delivered because it's too much for one man to carry."

Penny rolls her eyes. This is feeling more like the Penny I know and I'm beginning to let my guard down.

When we reach the grocery store the parking lot is packed. I cringe at the thought of what the interior is going to be like. Penny obviously noticing my reluctance picks up a handful of snow from the piles mounted along the parking lot. She skillfully forms it into a ball and throws it at me hitting me full in the chest. She then throws her arms up in a V shape, in the universal sign for touchdown, and shouts, "Score one for the good guys."

"Okay, slugger, game on," I say and begin to pelt her with one snowball after another.

After a few minutes of an all-out frontal attack she signals for timeout. "I surrender," she says and falls into my arms causing us both to fall onto a snow bank. We both explode in gales of laughter. I haven't laughed that hard since—since I can't remember when.

Inside the grocery store I push the cart while Penny makes the food selections. It's almost as though she never left I muse as I watch her squeeze the bread and check the expiration dates on the canned goods.

"We're going to need two baskets," I say as the grocery cart threatens to overflow.

"I'm almost done," Penny says as she sets a bag of potatoes on the under carriage next to a large package of paper towels.

On the way out of the parking lot we stop and purchase a tree from the Boy Scout Christmas tree lot. It's a Colorado Blue Spruce, Penny's and my favorite evergreen. It's in a bucket with a ball of dirt around the base. "We can plant this outside this spring," Penny says. "It will be the start of our new life together."

I nod and try not to react to Penny's nonchalant attitude in light of all that's happened. I'm still overwhelmed by the recent developments and don't want to get my hopes up. My heart says one thing; my mind says something else. The small voice within me says, "How can you help but not love this woman. What do you have to lose by giving it another try?"

While at the mall we run into one of the reporters from the *Erie Chronicle*. We recognize each other and she also seems to have recognized Penny. She has a strange look on her face. "How you two doing?" she asks.

"Just doing some last minute Christmas shopping," I say as she continues to eye Penny.

After a while Penny asks, "Do I know you?"

The reporter replies, "I'm Lela McKinsey. I'm a reporter with the *Erie Chronicle.*" She extends her hand to Penny and the two exchange greetings.

"I'm sorry," I say. "I should have introduced the two of you." To Lela I say, "This is my wife Penny."

Lela's chin drops and she appears to be speechless. *Odd for a reporter!* "But…I thought—"

"That I was deceased?" Penny fills in the blanks. "Word of my death was greatly exaggerated. Denny and I were just separated and I went to live with some friends in Canada and Denny and I are now back together."

Lela was one of my most avid critics. She made it clear that she didn't think the death penalty was good enough for me. And neither did her editor or anyone else at the newspaper for that matter.

The article appearing in the *Erie Chronicle* the next morning reads:

ANOTHER OF BALLARD'S "VICTIMS" RISES FROM THE DEAD

Penny Ballard, the wife of businessman Denton Ballard and the subject of an intensive police investigation is very much alive. She was seen by a reporter from the *Erie Chronicle* on Friday Christmas shopping at the mall with her husband.

In a conversation with the reporter, Mrs. Ballard stated she and her husband had been separated and she had been living in Canada with friends. She said the two had now reconciled.

Denton Ballard, a local author and owner of Azar Publishers, had reported his wife Penny missing in March of last year, the day he returned from a business trip. That generated a manhunt culminating in first degree murder charges being filed against him. An El Paso County jury later found him not guilty of the charge.

Ballard had also been charged with first degree murder in connection with the disappearance of another woman, Twyla Marin, a longtime employee at Azar Publishers. The charges were dismissed in the middle of trial when Marin appeared in court and was recognized by a witness for the prosecution.

Ballard spent the better part of nine months in the Boulder County jail awaiting trial in the two cases. From the beginning he had proclaimed his innocence and had passed polygraph exams in both cases. District Attorney Arthur Debow, the prosecutor in both cases, declined to comment.

I turn to the editorial page. Sure enough there's an editorial concerning Penny's return. It's titled, RETURN ENGAGEMENT. What a difference a year makes. I'm now heralded a hero. Interesting! Same editor, different assessment.

Denton Ballard spent nine long months in jail awaiting trial for not one but two murders he didn't commit. Both of the so called victims as it turns out are very much alive. Mr. Ballard's wife, Penny, has returned from a 'leave of absence' and is back with her husband. The *Erie Chronicle* wonders what would have happened had Mr. Ballard been found guilty in the two cases and received the death penalty.

Without a body and no real proof that the two women were dead, the prosecution proceeded. Fortunately for Mr. Ballard the jury in the so-called death of his wife found him not guilty and in the second case upon return of the victim the case was dismissed.

The two cases have something else in common. Both were presented by the prosecution to a grand jury to see if charges should be brought.

The evidence to indict was slight and an indictment does away with a screening device called a preliminary hearing. Had the case proceeded to a preliminary hearing, it is doubtful a trained judge would have found probable cause. Our question is why our elected district attorney chose to take the cases before a grand jury. One can only speculate.

Several months pass and Penny and I are still in the same bedroom but not in the same bed. I try to curb my suspicions. She apparently developed a drinking habit while she was gone and spends more and more time "out with the girls." I temper my urge to confront her but I don't want to appear accusatory.

One day when I leave work a little early and unexpectedly arrive home I walk in on Penny and her riding companion, Thelma Jorgensen, sitting at the kitchen table giggling and clinking glasses. Open in front of them is an almost empty bottle of vodka.

"Come join us," Thelma begs.

"We're drinking some coping juice," Penny says and holds up the almost empty bottle. "Want to try some of this?"

Although I'm disgusted at having found two intoxicated women at my kitchen table in the middle of the day I try to be cordial. "What are we celebrating?" I ask not knowing what else to say.

The ice tinkles as Thelma holds up her glass and tips it in a mock salute toward Penny. "Penny's return home," she slurs.

I join them at the table but pass on the vodka. Looking directly into Penny's eyes, I say, "You've been doing that for several months now."

"Don't be a party pooper," Penny says and leans into me waving the bottle in my face. "Try it, you might like it!" It's then I realize I underestimated Penny's degree of drunkenness. Her flip attitude is much out of character.

I gently push her hand holding the bottle away from my face and say, "Have and don't. I don't like the taste and don't like the effect."

"Aw, come on," Thelma chimes in. "It takes a while to get used to."

"Thanks anyway, think I'll pass. That's not something I want to get used to." I rise and head for the computer room amid their hysterical laughter.

That night Penny is unruly. Among other things, she accuses me of being a stick in the mud and insulting her in front of her friend. When the exchange between us becomes ugly, in order to avoid the inevitable bitter argument, I spend the night on the sofa in the den.

The next day I get a call from our bank. "Your joint account is overdrawn," the bookkeeper says.

I'm shocked. We always kept a significant amount on hand. "By how much?"

"Twenty-two hundred dollars," the bookkeeper nonchalantly replies.

Holy crap! Overdrawn by over two thousand dollars? "That can't be," I say. "I just transferred thirty-five hundred dollars from my savings account."

"Yes, sir, I see that entry in the ledger. However your balance, as of today, shows you're overdrawn. If you would like to come by the bank, I'll go over the transactions with you personally."

I'm livid but don't take it out on the bookkeeper. "Just close out the account and transfer any shortage from my savings account."

"Yes, sir. Sorry to be the bearer of bad news."

"Not your fault. You've been just great."

When I confront Penny, she says she loaned money to a friend and paid off some credit cards. She's not happy when I say I closed the joint account. When I left the office I went by the bank and opened a checking account in just my name. Out of it I pay our living expenses. I have no idea what she did with the $100,000 she took from the home safe. When I talk about the need for a budget she becomes enraged. To avoid a confrontation I don't bring up the subject again.

Several days later I receive another shock when a hysterical female calls my office and tells me Penny is having an affair with the woman's husband. She refuses to identify herself. "I followed the rotten son-of-a-bitch when he left the house this morning. He's at your house as we speak. His pickup is parked in your driveway." The caller hangs up without saying anything more.

I have no reason not to believe the caller. I slam the phone down and race to my car. I put the pedal to the metal and ignore the speed limit as I make a beeline for home. I'm beyond fed-up. Penny can pack up her belongings and get the hell out of my life—this time forever. I'll have Will or someone from his firm serve her with divorce papers.

The element of surprise is always an advantage so upon arrival at home I go in through the back door. Two empty glasses and an empty bottle of Ketel One vodka are sitting on the kitchen counter. I tiptoe past the counter and when I do so I muse that Penny serves Thelma Smirnoff and saves the expensive stuff for her lover. As I cross the kitchen I hear laughter coming from the family room. I quietly approach the doorway and when I peer inside I see what I envisioned in my mind many times—Penny making love to a man I don't recognize. Enraged I step into the room and pull the naked man off Penny. He strikes me with his fist and while I attempt to recover he grabs his clothes and heads out the door. Penny sits up and uses her arms to cover her breasts. Glaring at me she says, "I thought you were in Denver today."

I gently rub my chin where I took the blow. I'm abashed at her comment and lash out at her. "Apparently so! Is that all you can say? How long has this been going on and who the hell is the Casanova with the cobra tattooed on his ass?"

I'm further enraged when Penny answers so matter-of-factly, "No one you'd know." She stands and puts on her clothes and starts to leave the room.

I catch her by the shoulder and swing her toward me. "Not so damn fast! Don't you think you owe me and explanation?"

She pushes me away and shouts, "F- - - off! I don't *owe* you anything!"

She closes the door in my face and I pursue her. I grab her arm when I catch up to her and pulling free, she snatches a figurine from the top of the hall table and hurls it at me. It hits me above the eye and I feel blood gush from the wound. Infuriated, I reach for her and as she jerks away from my grasp she falls backwards hitting her head on the newel post supporting the bannister leading to the upstairs bedrooms.

Penny lies motionless at the foot of the stairs and I rush to her. I'm afraid to move her for fear I'd cause her further injury. I dial 911 and as I wait for the ambulance I get a cold washcloth and clean the blood from her head hoping to revive her. I search her wrist but can't find a pulse. I fear the worst.

When I hear the ambulance coming up the driveway I swing the front door open and stand aside giving the emergency responders room to operate. The EMT's have no better luck locating a pulse. Manipulating a stethoscope around on Penny's chest, one of the EMTs says, "I can't find a heartbeat." Although no one says the words, I instinctively know Penny is gone.

I'm allowed to sit on the bench next to Penny on the way to the hospital. One of the EMTs stays by her side continuing to administer CPR and monitors her but she doesn't show any signs of life. Upon arrival at the hospital Penny is immediately rushed to the ER and I stand helplessly by watching a team of medical personnel work feverishly over her. After long minutes of administering all the known heroics to save a life the attending physician straightens and turns to me.

"You the patient's husband?" he asks as he places his stethoscope around his neck.

"Yes." I feel my knees grow weak as my stomach churns.

"I'm sorry to inform you that we were too late to save her." The doctor looks back at Penny's body lying on the examination table and I break down and sob uncontrollably. The doctor takes my elbow and ushers me out into the corridor. He pats me on the back and then disappears into another examination room.

OMG! What do I do now? How am I going to explain this to Penny's family and mine? I call Penny's parents first. When I explain what happened they're horrified. "Wasn't your fault," Penny's father manages to say. Her mother echoes the same sentiment. Their grief and shock are evident in their voices and I can barely keep my voice steady. I no more than end the call when Fuller and Whittaker appear on the scene.

"You two never give up, do you?" I say and damn the consequences. I'm sick and tired of being dogged by these two.

"Just doing our job," Fuller says.

"Do you have a minute to talk?" Whittaker asks.

We find a quiet corner and I relate the full story including the anonymous phone call. From previous experience, I can tell they don't believe me.

"Mind if we follow you home and have a look around?" Fuller asks.

"And if I say no?"

"Then we'll get a search warrant," Fuller says.

"Don't bother," I say. "There's not much to see but have at it."

I'm not allowed to move or touch Penny until an autopsy is performed. Fuller and Whittaker follow me home. After all, what do I have to hide.

The cops pull up behind me and the minute we arrive, my residence is treated like a crime scene. Crime scene tape is used to cordon off several rooms of the house. I'm grateful the yellow CRIME SCENE DO NOT CROSS tape is not strewn across the entrance to the house.

As I explain what happened and where it happened, I'm instructed by Fuller not to touch anything. The figurine smeared with my blood and Penny's fingerprints is still lying where it landed after it hit me above the eye. After Whittaker photographs the figurine he is ordered by Fuller to take photos of my wound. While I'm posing for Whittaker, the crime scene investigators arrive and begin collecting their samples. "We'll need to get a blood sample from you," Fuller says to me.

The washcloth I used to wipe the blood from Penny's head is collected along with blood samples from the post where Penny hit her head. DNA samples are taken from the family room along with fingerprints. Fingerprints are also removed from the two glasses and the vodka bottle on the kitchen counter.

When Whittaker is finished taking photographs he joins Fuller and me at the kitchen table.

"How is it you came home early from the office? We know you're in the habit of working late," Fuller says.

"Like I told Deputy Whittaker, I received a call from a woman who said her husband was having an affair with Penny and that the two were at my home as we spoke. She also said I would find his pickup parked in my driveway."

"Did the woman identify herself?" Fuller persists.

"No, and when I asked who she was she instantly hung up."

"After you received the call, what did you do?"

"I immediately drove home of course."

"What time did you arrive at home?"

"I didn't look at my watch. I would say it was somewhere around two or two fifteen. It only takes about fifteen minutes to go from my office to my home."

"What did you do when you got home?"

"I parked the car and went around back and came in the house through the back door. I then heard laughter coming from the family room. That's where I encountered Penny and a man I'd never seen before engaged in the sexual act."

When tears form, Fuller hands me a tissue. "I'm sorry I say," as I wipe my eyes.

After a few moments Fuller continues with her interview. "When you interrupted their fun, what happened?"

"I jerked the man off of Penny. He struck me with his fist here," I point to my face, "on the chin." Fuller gives me a quick once over. I guess I'm pretty much a mess with having been slugged by Casanova and then clobbered with the figurine by

Penny. I continue, "The man then gathered his clothes and headed to the other end of the house and out the door."

"Un-huh. What did Penny do?"

"She just sat there naked with her arms covering her breasts."

"Did she say anything?"

"Yes, she said she thought I was in Denver."

"What did you say?"

"I was flabbergasted at her nonchalant remark. I asked her if that was all she could say? I then asked her who the Casanova with the cobra tattoo on his ass was."

"Was there a tattoo of a cobra on his ass?"

Fuller looks at me like she thinks I made that up? "There was!" I want to suggest they collect forensic evidence at the autopsy that might identify the mystery man as well as run the cobra tattoo through their data bank. How many guys would have a cobra tattooed on their butt?

"Did you recognize the man?"

"No, never saw him before."

"After you asked your wife who the man was, what did she say?"

"Something like, 'No one you'd know."

"What happened next?"

"When Penny dressed and started to leave the room, I grabbed her by the shoulder and swung her around. 'Don't you think you owe me an explanation?' I asked." I pause and rub what's left of my face with my hands as I remember my last moments with Penny. Tears threaten again but I fight them back. "She pushed me away and told me to F--- off."

"And were you still in the family room?"

"We were."

"What happened next?"

"She ran out of the room slamming the door in my face. I kicked it open and tried to catch up to her. As I closed the gap between us, she turned and grabbed a figurine from the hall table and flung it at me. It hit me above the eye." I point to the spot that is now swollen. "With blood streaming in my eye I grabbed for her and when she jerked away she fell backwards and hit her head on the post at the bottom of the stairway."

"Did you administer first aid?"

"I was afraid to move her and immediately called 911. When I couldn't find a pulse I got a cold washcloth and tried to revive her. It was shortly thereafter that the EMTs arrived."

The interview with my two nemeses left me unnerved but I blew it off as paranoia. However, they did leave the crime scene tape attached when they departed which was not a good omen.

It isn't until I read the article in the morning edition of the *Erie Chronicle* that I decide I'd better call Will.

DEATH OF LOCAL RESIDENT BEING INVESTIGATED

> An autopsy was scheduled today for Penny Ballard, wife of local businessman Denton Ballard, in what appears to have been an accidental death. Mrs. Ballard was rushed to the ER at Erie General late yesterday afternoon after a fall at the family residence. The incident is currently under investigation by the Boulder County Sheriff's Office.

"If you hadn't called me, I'd be calling you," Will says. "Just read about Penny's unfortunate accident. My condolences."

"At least everyone so far is considering Penny's fall an accident. With Fuller and Whittaker assigned the investigation, who knows how the fall will be construed."

"Maybe we should meet before the matter gets out of control," Will suggests. "Hold on while I check my calendar." Will's soon back on the line, "I have an open appointment at ten if that works for you."

"See you at ten."

When I meet with Will I relate the circumstances of Penny's death. He shakes his head.

"Am I in trouble?"

"Depends on whether Debow learned his lesson in the first two trials. My gut tells me that with Fuller and Whittaker involved you might be facing criminal charges."

OMG! Here we go again. "You've got to be kidding."

"Not in the least, I wouldn't do that to you after all you've been through. With yours and Penny's history there's no telling what theory they might hatch. The good news is that jeopardy attached when you were acquitted for having killed Penny. You can't be tried twice for the same offense. That would be double jeopardy and a violation of the Fifth Amendment."

Before I leave Will promises to obtain a copy of the autopsy report and stay in touch with the DA's office to try to head off any criminal prosecution should Debow be so predisposed. "Debow, like every prosecutor in the country is familiar with the double jeopardy provision in the Constitution and I can't imagine he would jeopardize his reelection bid by another stupid act," Will says.

The next day Will calls and advises me of the results of the autopsy. "The county coroner attributes death to 'blunt trauma

174

to the cranium consistent with a fall or being hit with a heavy instrument.'"

My hopes that I would be vindicated are dashed. "Guess that leaves open the possibility that I might have hit her."

"There is that! But the blood on the post at the bottom of the stairway and Penny lying in close proximity seems to refute that."

"Think Debow may be pressured by his flunkies, Fuller and Whittaker, to file criminal charges?"

"Possible but very unlikely. We'll soon find out. I ran into Debow at the courthouse and he said he'd allow you to turn yourself in if charges are filed. I have no indication whether he will or won't."

...allow me to turn myself in! How generous. Maybe I'll disappear...

A week passes before I hear from Will.

"Bad news?" I ask before we exchange greetings.

"Afraid so," Will says. "Had a jury trial continued so I'm free anytime you are."

"Ten?"

"You're on!"

Almost as soon as I'm ushered into Will's office he hands me a criminal complaint. It charges me with second degree murder, manslaughter and criminally negligent homicide."

My legs fail me and I collapse into the nearest chair. "Yikes!"

"You can't be convicted of all three. The last two are lesser included of second degree murder."

Well, gee, that's a relief.

Will pulls out a volume of the Colorado statutes. "*Knowingly* causing the death of a person is second degree murder. The penalty is eight to twenty-four years. *Recklessly* causing the death of a person is manslaughter. The penalty is two to six years. Causing death by *criminal negligence* is criminally negligent homicide and carries a penalty of one to three years."

"Whether I'm sentenced to twenty-four, six or three years depends on whether what I did was done knowingly, recklessly or negligently, correct?"

"*Knowingly* means that you were aware that your conduct was practically certain to cause the result. *Recklessly* means you consciously disregarded a substantial and unjustifiable risk that the result would occur. *Criminal negligence* means you failed to perceive a substantial and unjustifiable risk that the result would occur."

"If I deliberately pushed Penny into the railing, would that be second degree murder?"

"Probably."

"If I just pushed her, would that be manslaughter?"

"Probably."

"What if I just reached for her and she pulled away and fell backwards?"

"Could be criminal negligence but in all likelihood it would be nothing since it was an accident."

I scratch my head. Will squints at me.

"Why are you looking at me like that?" I ask.

"Because I told you you've already been tried for Penny's death and acquitted. You can't be tried again—no matter what the circumstances are."

"Then why is Debow pursuing it?"

"You'll have to ask him."

At the arraignment I plead not guilty and ask for a jury trial. In my behalf, Will also asks for a preliminary hearing.

At the preliminary hearing, the presiding judge finds probable cause or reasonable cause to believe I caused Penny's death and the case is bound over to district court for trial. District Court Judge Beth Robbins has been assigned to the case.

At the motions hearing Will moves to dismiss the case based on the Fifth Amendment. "Mr. Ballard has already been tried and acquitted for the murder of his wife. He can't be tried again. To do so would be to place him in jeopardy twice for the same offense."

Debow argues that the offenses are different. "In the first case, Mr. Ballard was charged with first degree murder. In this case he has been charged with second degree murder."

When Will starts to stand to offer rebuttal, Judge Robbins motions for him to remain seated. "Mr. Debow," she begins, "I don't know what law school you went to but it sounds like they didn't either teach you very well or that you didn't pay attention." The judge slides her glasses up to reposition them and glares at Debow. "I suspect it was the latter. Basic to our whole system of criminal justice is the concept that a district attorney can't keep prosecuting an accused for the same crime over and over again until he or she gets a conviction."

Out of the corner of my eye I watch Debow slide lower in his chair.

Judge Robbins continues, "To do so, Mr. Debow, is a violation of the United States Constitution as well as the Colorado Constitution. As Mr. Crowley says, 'It's double jeopardy.' Your assertion that first degree murder and second degree murder are not the same for jeopardy to apply is an absurdity. Second degree murder is a lesser included offense of first degree murder. Manslaughter is a lesser included offense of second degree murder and criminally negligent homicide is a lesser included offense of manslaughter. That means that once an accused has been tried and acquitted of the greater offense he or she has been tried and acquitted of the lesser included offenses as well."

Judge Robbins rears back in her chair with blood in her eyes. When Debow starts to argue with her she says, "I don't want to rule in your favor and get reversed. Otherwise, I'd look as stupid as you. For the forgoing reasons, the court rules in defendant's favor. The charges against Mr. Ballard are hereby dismissed—with prejudice! What that means, Mr. Debow, they can never be re-filed."

What a reprimand. I want to stand and applaud.

Will whispers, "No love lost there."

"What do you think his reelection chances are?"

"If I was one of his deputies, I'd be looking for a new job," Will says and grins from ear to ear. However, neither of us laugh. Nothing is funny anymore.

12

FOREVER AFTER

After the dismissal of the charges in Penny's death there were some who scoffed at the idea of murder charges being dismissed on the basis of a technicality. The editorial in the *Erie Chronicle* only added fuel to the fire. I clipped it and saved it thinking I might use it in a future novel. It read:

A FLAWED SYSTEM OF JUSTICE

I believe in the Constitution and I think most Americans do. It was ratified by the states in 1789—thirteen years after the Declaration of Independence. It together with the Bill of Rights (the first ten amendments to the constitution adopted two years later) is considered the supreme law of the land. All well and good!

What the editorial staff of the *Erie Chronicle* takes issue with is that portion of the Fifth Amendment called the double jeopardy clause that allows a man to kill his wife without any repercussion. The Ballard case is a prime example.

There are others in the community who think much like the *Erie Chronicle* and who can't make up their minds as to whether I'm a goat or a hero. There's an old Bible verse that says, *Judge not least ye be judged.* And another that says, *Let he who is without fault cast the first stone.* I have been convicted in the court of public opinion on numerous occasions and have been vindicated in a court of law on each occasion. Apparently that doesn't appease the naysayers. Guess I know who my friends are by who stuck by me through some extremely difficult times. My enemies will never be with me. My friends will always be with me.

When people ask me how I'm doing, I tell them I feel like Humpty Dumpty after his great fall. No matter how hard I try, I can't seem to put all the pieces of my life back together. At least not like they were before I cheated on Penny. Even though I've been legally vindicated of all criminal charges, I cannot find it in my heart to forgive myself for my indiscretions and the hurt I caused the woman I loved. Penny's final days on this earth were not happy ones due in no small part to my philandering ways. I take responsibility for her death and ask for God's forgiveness.

I prayed I would receive some sign from above that Penny had forgiven me. My prayers were answered when I awoke one morning to find Kamanda in my bed tucked in next to me. I detected a smile on Kamanda's face and thought I heard Penny singing our favorite song, *Turn Back to Me*.

As I pen this I'm at a book signing at Barnes & Noble with my latest novel. When I'm not working, I'm writing. The name of my latest novel? *Kamanda*.

ABOUT THE AUTHORS

JUDITH BLEVINS' WHOLE professional life has been centered in and around the courts and the criminal justice system. Her experience in having been a court clerk and having served under five consecutive district attorneys in Grand Junction, Colorado, has provided the fodder for her novels. She has had a daily dose of mystery, intrigue and courtroom drama over the years and her novels share all with her readers.

CARROLL MULTZ, A trial lawyer for over forty years, a former two-term district attorney, assistant attorney general, and judge, has been involved in cases ranging from municipal courts to and including the United States Supreme Court. His high profile cases have been reported in the *New York Times*, *Redbook Magazine* and various police magazines. He was one of the attorneys in the Columbine Copycat Case that occurred in Fort Collins, Colorado, in 2001 that was featured by Barbara Walters on ABC's *20/20*. Now retired, he is an Adjunct Professor at Colorado Mesa University in Grand Junction, Colorado, teaching law-related courses at both the graduate and undergraduate levels.

CPSIA information can be obtained
at www.ICGtesting.com
Printed in the USA
FSHW011015261218

9 781948 540704